To

Deven

Love

[signature]

Follow your dreams!

POPULAR OUTSIDERS

Shamiya Marshae

Copyright © 2017 by Shamiya Marshae Pasquet

Book Cover by Shamiya Marshae Pasquet

Interior Designs and Graphics by Shamiya Marshae Pasquet

ISBN-13: 978-0-692-93460-9

ISBN-10: 0-692-93460-9

Dedicated to all the popular outsiders. You're not alone.

&

Dedicated to my Mom, Sister and grandfather, who've always encouraged and believed in me. None of this would be possible without them. I Love you.

A Popular Outsider,

Both noticed and ignored,

Often envied by most,

But never comforted,

Few choose to be themselves,

Few can be themselves,

But that's what makes a Popular Outsider

unique.

CHAPTER ONE

Popular Outsiders

In RoseOak you were either popular or an outsider. Like the Rose, the town was beautiful, but it also had its thorns. Residents of the town liked to hide their thorns, though. No one *truly* knew each other in the town and no one had attempted to try. They all were wrapped in their own lives, so they couldn't be bothered with others. A town both known and unknown. Known for the people that made it out, making something of themselves. Unknown for the people who stayed, forgotten along with the town. Growing up in RoseOak could be both easy and hard. The town was small and seemed to always be filled with trivial gossip.

There wasn't room for mistakes or flaws, because they would always be used against you. Making you either on the town's good or bad side. Neither one was enjoyable. Being on the good side meant working even harder to stay there, it meant living your life by the town's expectations and not your own. However, the bad side was just as miserable. The bad side was solely there for those the town deemed unworthy. They were shunned and often taunted. Being on the bad side meant living the way you wanted to, but with the prospect of living that life alone.

There were few who fell in the in between of those two classes. Those who were both high and low. Content and depressed. They were the ones that everyone noticed, but also the ones no one actually knew. They were the *Popular Outsiders*.

The sky was grey, adding to the gloomy atmosphere. Lightning flashed and thunder rang out, signaling it was going to rain soon. In the corner of the small room, a girl jumped. The boy sitting across from her shook his head and slouched further into his seat. The door opened, grabbing everyone's attention. They were both disappointed to see another student, yet again.

Her ponytail swished from side to side, as she strutted to her seat. She smirked at the attention that was on her. Her happiness was cut short, once her eyes fell upon the girl in the corner. The other girl held her gaze for a moment, before breaking eye contact. She smiled at the girl's intimidation and sat down. Her eyes ran over the girl's attire and she giggled. "What are you wearing?! Let your mother dress you, *again*?" The girl kept her head down and didn't respond.

The cheerleader's jaw clenched and she snapped her fingers "Hey, I'm talking to you." The boy spoke from beside her "Leave her alone, Madison. She isn't bothering you." Her head snapped in his direction and she frowned "I don't believe I was talking to *you*, Ace, now was I? And I'd be careful with challenging me. We all know what happens to those that do." she finished with a wave of her phone. Ace released a breath, before turning in his seat, giving up. He had tried, but if the girl was going to continue to let Madison pick on her and not stand up for herself, he couldn't help her. Besides, he had enough problems of his own.

Madison turned to taunt the other girl some more, but was stopped by the door opening. A boy walked in, followed by a girl. Both were the complete opposites of each other. One rich, one poor. One pampered, one neglected. One popular, one an outsider. They were having a discussion about something. The expressions on their faces showed that it must be something serious.

"Josh!" Madison called from her seat. A seductive smile covered her lips, as she beckoned him over. Josh returned the smile and made his way over to her. The conversation he had been having with Courtney, now forgotten. Courtney's shoulders fell, as she watched the scene in front of her. Ace gave her a sympathetic smile and patted the chair next to his. She placed on a forced smile and made her way over to him. Once she sat down, he turned to her. He glanced at Josh and shook his head "He's not worth it." She sighed "You don't understand. He...We..." she gave up trying to explain and sighed, again. She looked at Josh and spoke in a whisper "It's complicated."

Ace frowned and opened his mouth to say more, but once again, the door opened. Amber walked into the room, her eyes searching for a seat. She froze upon spotting the last available one or more so the person near it. Amber made her way to the seat, trying to ignore Ace presence. Who couldn't help, but stare at her. It had been two weeks since the two of them had been in the same room, together. Amber greeted Courtney and pulled out a textbook from her bag. She was most likely studying for a test that was two months away. *As usual*. Ace turned back around to face the front.

The clock ticking was the only sound that could be heard in the silent room. Conversations had stopped. The six teens had begun to feel anxious, as more time passed by. None of them knew why they had been suddenly called to the Counselor's office. Some expected the worse, while others couldn't care less.

The door opened. Each one of them watched in hopes of it not being another student. A disheveled woman rushed into the classroom. Her arms were full of papers and a briefcase rested on her shoulder. She scurried to her desk and let the papers fall onto it. Her hand pushed back the hair falling into her face and she released a heavy breath "Sorry I'm late."

No one said anything. They were used to the strange counselor by now. Ms. Clover looked around the room and smiled. She cleared her throat, adjusting her suit. "Well, I see you all have made it. Now, let's get to business." The bell rang. Some of the teens groaned, not liking the idea of missing class.

Ms. Clover sat in her chair and clasped her hands together on the desk. A serious expression took over her face. "Now, I know you all are wondering why you're here." She held up some of the papers. "Well, it seems all of you have the same problem. To put it all simply, all of you are missing the volunteer hours needed to graduate. Which means if you do not make them up by the end of the year, you will not be graduating." All of them now sat straight in their seats, eyes wide. "But, do not fret. I do have a solution to all of your problems." Ms. Clover flicked through the stack of papers, before pulling a sheet out and holding it up.

She sighed at their blank faces and placed the poster down. "I know this might not be something you all like, but it's the only solution. It's either do this or don't graduate. Mr. Jones is a very wise man, you might even learn a couple things from him. Besides, it gives you all the chance to bond and make new friendships, before the year is over."

The teens were silent. Lightning flashed and thunder clapped. Rain began to fall. The pitter-patter of rain droplets hit the window in a rhythm. It was both calming and nerve-wrecking.

Madison raised her hand and Ms. Clover motioned for her to speak. "So, what you're saying is we have to do this or we don't graduate. Isn't there anything else available?" Ms. Clover shook her head "Sadly, no. Everything else is either full or over. You would have to wait until next year." The cheerleader scowled "How many hours are we missing, can't you just ignore it?"

"With that being both against school rules and unfair, I am afraid I cannot do that."

The cheerleader fell back into her seat and crossed her arms.

Courtney shrugged and spoke up "Well, I don't feel like spending any extra time in high school, so I'm in." The rest of the teens slowly, nodded their heads, also agreeing. Ms. Clover smiled and stood up, she walked around the desk and proceeded to pass out some papers.

"Great! Just fill these papers out. You all will meet with Mr. Jones at his farm, every afternoon, around four o'clock." The cheery counselor stood back to analyze the students. "I'm sure you guys are going to enjoy this. I think this would be good for you all. Who knows? This experience just might change all of you."

Don't look at the outside people often display,

Because that is never the truth,

The truth lies beneath all of that,

And it takes a special shovel to dig through all those layers,

A special shovel called trust.

CHAPTER TWO

Beneath it all

The bell rang and that's when the stampede began. It was lunchbreak, but it was also Monday, which meant it was Sub Day. There were only two days out the week students fought to get to the cafeteria like this. Mondays and Fridays. Sub days and Pizza days. Amber was the last to leave the classroom, just as she was always the first to enter. Today had been different, though. Her perfect attendance had been broken. She had forgotten that the school required a hundred hours of community service in order to graduate. Now, she had yet another thing to add to her list of stress.

Her finger twitched, but she pushed the feeling away. It was not the time for any of that. She had to focus. There was only a few months left in the school year until it was over. That wouldn't stop her from working hard, though. She was top of all of her classes and if she was going to stay there, she couldn't let anything distract her.

"Amber!"

Speaking of distractions. Amber turned around coming faced to face with the very person she had been trying to avoid. For the past two weeks she had been successful, but that ended today. "Yes, Ace." He sighed at the look she was giving him and motioned toward the lockers. "Can we talk for a moment?" Together, they walked to the lockers, away from the prying ears of other students.

Amber crossed her arms waiting for him to speak. "You've been avoiding me." Her eyebrow raised "Can you blame me?" With a breath of frustration, Ace spoke again "For the last time, Amber. Madison lied. I didn't cheat on you." He was telling the truth and Amber could tell. She looked away, knowing if she looked any longer she would take him back. "It doesn't matter, Ace. That's not the only problem. But, it's over. We're over." She tried to walk away, but he grabbed her arm, stopping her arm.

"Then what is the problem? Tell me, I'll fix it." Amber shook her head, not being able to speak. Her emotions were starting to get the best of her. Pulling her arm from his grasp, she turned around, walking in a hurry down the hall. She only slowed her pace, once she rounded the corner. Amber hated that she had to treat Ace this way, but it was for the best. For both her and Ace. With all she had going on and college only a few months away, she didn't have time for a boyfriend or the other things teens her age liked to entertain themselves with. She had dreams to fulfill, even if they weren't her own.

Amber was almost to her classroom, when she was stopped. She looked from the hand on her shoulder to its owner. Mr. Banks gave her a smile "Ah...Just the person I wanted to see. This is the student I was telling you all about." Amber gave a small smile to the three adults standing in front of her. Mr. Banks wore a huge smile on his face, as he spoke. After a couple of minutes, Amber tuned the adults out, the thing she did in most cases similar to this one. To her parents and the school's staff, she was like a trophy. A prized possession, they liked to flaunt around. She was always told what to do or what was needed of her. Her life revolved around satisfying everyone else's lives.

"Amber? Are you alright?"

She looked up meeting their concerned eyes. *I wonder if they genuinely care*. A forced smile appeared on her lips. *They couldn't tell the difference*. "I'm fine. Just dazed off for a moment." Relief showed in Mr. Banks eyes. He placed a hand on her shoulder and shook his head "Good. I was worried for a second. Try not to daze off too much, though. We wouldn't want to lose one of our top students." he finished with a laugh and his colleagues followed suit. Amber laughed, also. None of them noticing her finger nails digging into her notebook.

The warning bell rang. Mr. Banks looked up and sighed. "Well, I'm not going to keep you here. Don't want you missing class." Amber gave them all a smile and greeting, before heading to class.

As she walked, she could feel the familiar urges start to kick in. Her pace picked up and her fingers tapped vigorously on her notebook. Her mind was bombarded with thoughts urging her to do it, while her brain tried to protest. Her master was both her enemy and friend, it took more than it gave. But, she saw no wrong in the things her master did to her. After all, her master helped her achieve levels of happiness no one else was able to give her. It gave her moments of peace and in the end, that was all she wanted, even if it meant losing a little of her sanity bit by bit.

Finally, it was lunch break. The students exited their classrooms in a stampede, most of them meeting up with friends. The school year was closing in, so everyone had already formed their designated cliques. All accept one.

Bambi walked down the hall, her eyes casted to the ground. She was similar to the students that hid in the school's corners or ate lunch alone. There was only one thing that set her apart from them. She was noticed.

Bambi tried her best to be unseen, to blend in with everyone else, but she always failed. She would wear oversized hoodies and throw her hair in a messy ponytail, but some days were different. Days like this. Today, she wore the new outfit her mother had gotten her and made her hair look presentable. Dressing up made her mom happy and a part of it delighted her as well. The only downside was the attention she got from it.

Boys would always be boys, so of course they flirted and complimented. She took none of them serious, though. She knew there was only one thing they had in mind. That made her feel worse. The fact, that they were only interested in her for her looks. None of them had tried to get to know her. Most of them had their minds set on what they thought of her. Their sources being false rumors and petty gossip.

The girls were worse than the guys, though. Their words were solely used to tear her apart. They berated and criticized every aspect of her. And she believed every single word.

There had been countless times when she had gone to bed. Their taunts still on her mind. She wondered if she fixed her *problems* would they then like her. Would the taunts stop? Would they accept her? She knew the answer to those questions already, so she settled for pushing away all her thoughts and feelings. Hoping not to trouble anyone else.

The cafeteria was just as clustered, as the hallway. The lines seeming endless. Each table held a different group of friends, voices raised trying to be heard over the boisterous cafeteria.

Bambi side-stepped pass horse playing boys and unmindful girls, trying not to be knocked over. She could feel her anxiety kicking in. Every morning she would think over scenarios, she knew most likely wouldn't happen.

Her pace quickened and she hoped no one thought her crazy. That would only make her more anxious. Her heart pounded, her chest rising and falling with each breath she took. She finally made it to the lunch line and tried to regulate her breathing. Doing what she was taught to do, she inhaled and exhaled deep, silent breaths.

Once she felt herself calm down, she took in her surroundings. It didn't seem as if anyone had noticed her ordeal and that relieved her. The line didn't look as if it was going to move anytime soon, so she opened the book that had been clutched to her chest and began to read. A joy and relaxation for her. She hadn't even read half of the page when someone interrupted her.

"Is it that good?"

Bambi's head shot up in alarm. She hated when people read her books over her shoulder. She didn't know why. It was just a pet peeve of hers. She looked at the boy and instantly recognized him. Who wouldn't? Josh was practically royalty in school. His father owned almost everything in RoseOak. Which earned Josh popularity, friendship, many girls' adorations for him and respect. She didn't know if it were all genuine, though.

She remembered his question and gave a simple nod. Josh didn't seem so bad, but she still didn't want him talking to her. He was on the highest level of popularity status and him talking to her would only make life for her harder. She started to turn away from him, but he spoke, again.

"So, you must like to read."

She again nodded. He placed his hands in his pockets "Really? What type of books?" She shrugged and didn't meet his eyes "Contemporary. Mostly romance and occasionally some fantasy." He stared at her for a moment, the corner of his lips quirking up "You don't like to talk that much, do you?" She shook her head.

He cocked his head to the side and looked her over "You really are beautiful, you know that?" She didn't. She didn't feel she was pretty at all and didn't see what guys saw in her, but she wouldn't tell him that. "Thank you." She responded politely.

He didn't say anything and she hoped he would finally leave her alone. Looking around her worries were correct. Girls were staring at the two of them. Some curious and other furious. She already knew how the rest of her day was going to turn out.

"I don't think you're like what everyone says you are." Bambi resisted the urge to frown. *Was this supposed to be his pick-up line?* If it was, she wasn't impressed. She had heard it all, before. Different ways and different times, but it was all the same in the end. It didn't matter if he didn't *think* she was like what the rumors implied, like all the others he probably *hoped* it was true.

She opened her mouth to respond, but was interrupted. "Well, what do we have here?" the familiar voice made her inwardly cringe. Bambi turned around, coming face to face with Madison. Every time they encountered one another, she wanted to ask the other girl why she hated her so much. The taunts had started with her, so maybe, she was the answer to all the questions she had. But, she knew that day would never come. She was far too intimidated by Madison and her friends.

Madison looked from Josh to Bambi and placed a hand on her hip "Trying to steal someone's boyfriend, again, Bambi?" she spoke in a scolding tone. No matter how quiet or invisible Bambi tried to be, Madison always sought her out.

Madison tilted her head. "Too ashamed to speak? Well, you should be. Plus, it's kind of embarrassing throwing yourself at someone like that. But, how would you know any better. When you're used to doing something, you kind of forget how wrong it is, right? And let's be honest this habit of yours has been going on for a while. Pretty sad if you ask me."

Surrounding students gave her looks of disgust and others grinned tauntingly. A few understood how Bambi was feeling and gave looks of sympathy, but none attempted to help. Josh watched the whole thing, silently. Madison smiled at him and placed a hand to his chest, fondly. "Sorry, you had to go through that. Just ignore girls like her. They're not any good." Bambi didn't speak on the fact that Madison was now doing the exact thing she had accused and scolded her for.

Josh looked from Madison's hand to Bambi. He shook his head and moved her hand away. "I have to go, see you later." He glanced at Bambi "Nice talking to you, Bambi." Without saying another word, he left.

Madison turned to glare at her, accusingly. Bambi didn't give her a chance to say anything else hurtful and pushed passed her and other students, exiting the cafeteria.

The school's stadium was emptied, as usual. The rain had stopped a couple hours earlier, but the bleachers and grass were still damp. She was far too dejected to care. Bambi walked over to the bleachers and sat, not caring that she was ruining her outfit. She'd deal with it later. Her stomach growled, but she ignored it. *Another day of not eating.*

The grey sky reflected how she felt on a daily basis. Blank. Her thoughts were like waves crashing down on her. Most of the time she would push her thoughts and feelings behind the many walls she had built. But one day, they were going to break through those walls. Engulfing her whole. The thought didn't scare her, though and that was what terrified her.

"Sorry, I didn't know anyone else came here, I'll go."

Bambi twisted around, but the boy was already turning to leave. She contemplated in her mind whether she should take a chance. Many of them hadn't gone well, but still she didn't give up.

"Wait!" He stopped, but didn't turn around. Bambi chewed on her lip for a moment "Um…you can sit here…I don't mind." He turned around and looked at her. His eyes left her and he walked back to the benches. He sat down and pulled out a brown paper bag, next appeared a sandwich.

Bambi's eyes locked on it and her stomach growled. The boy paused in unwrapping it and glanced at her stomach "You didn't eat?" she shook her head and waved him off "No, but it's alright. School's almost over any way."

He shook his head and broke off half of the sandwich, handing it to her. "Here. We still have two periods, left. You might pass out or something." Bambi took the sandwich from him. She thought of telling him that her body had already been trained to go a couple days without eating, but thought against it. She didn't want him labeling her anorexic or bulimic.

For a while, she stared at the sandwich. The boy took a bite out of his half and chuckled "It's not poisoned, I promise." Her eyes widened and she shook her head, vigorously. "N-No, it's not that. I'm just grateful." His eyebrow's furrowed, together and he shrugged "It's just a sandwich." Bambi nodded and took a bite. To him it might have seemed like a simple thing, but to her this small act of kindness meant a lot.

She knew what she was about to say could possibly backfire on her, but the most she would get hurt was her pride. And that had been hurt countless of times. She spoke, nervously "I'll bring you a lunch tomorrow." he paused "To…um…thank and repay you." he sighed "You don't have to do that." Bambi frowned "No, really, it's no big deal. I don't mind." He chuckled and went back to his sandwich "Okay. You win."

Bambi used the moments when he wasn't paying attention to look at him. He wasn't drop-dead gorgeous, but he wasn't unattractive either. He wore a sweater vest, paired with a pair of slacks. That and his glasses sat him apart from most of the guys at the school. That made her like him even more.

The bell rang and the boy's mood seemed to darken. Standing up, she gathered her trash and glanced at him. Bambi saw something in his eyes that surprised her. They were just like hers. They held the same emotions and told the same story. But, his looked a little darker. His flame was slowly diminishing.

The bench had caused her pants to get a little damp. She knew there were going to be some words said about it. Movement caught her attention. They boy stood up and removed his jacket. He handed it to her "Here, you can tie it around your waist"

Bambi nodded and took the jacket from him. He sat down, again and she frowned "Aren't you coming?" He shook his head "No. I think I'm going to stay out here a little longer." Bambi shrugged "Okay. Well, I guess I'll see you tomorrow. My name's Bambi, by the way." He gave her a small smile.

With that she left. Bambi was halfway back to the school's building when she realized something. She hadn't gotten his name. The warning bell rang and she pushed the thought away. She would just get his name tomorrow. Later, she would regret not going back.

Living to please people,

One of the most tiring things to do,

There's one person you never seem to please,

Yourself,

And that's the person,

You have to live with forever.

CHAPTER THREE

Pleasing Others

For most students the day was over and they would spend the rest of it at home, but that wasn't the case for Ace. School might have been over, but that was the start of practice. As the quarterback, it was his job to help lead and support the team. He walked into the locker room, slapping hands with some of his teammates.

"Man, can you believe it? After, this year's we'll no longer be high school students. We're going to have to start taking life serious. I don't know if I'm ready."

Maddox shoved Tatum and laughed "Dude, why are you being so dramatic?" Tatum shrugged and too, laughed "Don't know, but it is something to think about, you know?"

If anyone knew, it had to be Ace. The school year was ending soon. Which meant he had to make a decision that would dictate the rest of his life. Not only that, he now had to worry about earning his community service hours in order to graduate. The stress was slowly weighing in on him and the one person who was able to relieve him from it, barely acknowledged him.

Sometimes he had to question himself. Was all this worth it? All the long hours of work and short hours of rest. He didn't know the answer to the question. For once, he felt like a normal teen in this sense. Not knowing what he truly wanted out of life, but he knew he had to decide soon. He wasn't only trying to live his dreams. These dreams belonged to someone else and he felt the duty to do anything he can to fulfill them.

A whistle being blown brought him out of his thoughts. Coach Green stood in the doorway and analyzed them with hard eyes. He cared for all of them dearly, but when it came down to actual work, he showed them no mercy. His frown grew deeper and on cue, he began to shout "What are all of you doing?! How do you expect to beat Harlington like this?! Lying around and wasting the day!"

Their final game being against Harlington-their rival town is what made the game so anticipated. RoseOak hadn't lost to Harlington for twenty years straight, but this year their team was getting better. They had recruited some member from BlueShores, which Ace didn't think was fair, but he didn't think too hard on it. He was confident in his team and was sure their unbreakable record would remain untarnished.

"I want to see you all on the field by the count of three! One!-" His teammates scrambled to get out of the locker room. He was right behind them, but Coach's voice stopped him. "Wait just a moment, Ace. I'd like to speak with you." His friends gave him sympathetic looks, thinking he was in trouble. Ace inwardly groaned and followed Coach Green to the bleachers. He sat in front of him "Yes, Coach." The older man ran a hand down his face.

"One of the colleges had second thought and aren't offering you the scholarship, anymore." Ace's eyes widened and he sat up straighter "What?! Why?!" Coach stared at him for a moment. His look said he should already know the answer to his question. "Let's not beat around the bush, Ace. You haven't been yourself, lately. You're dropping the ball, Getting tackled, and it's like you've even forgotten how to throw a football. So, tell me. What's the problem, son."

He couldn't tell the truth. Coach would think he was crazy. He shrugged and gave an idle reply "I don't know." It was a lie. He had known what was causing his mishaps in football, for a while, now. Still, he didn't speak of it. The deadlines both near and distant was like a never-ending weight on his shoulders. Sometimes he wished the world would stop to give him time to catch up and wrap his head around things, but he knew that was impossible and too much to ask for. The world didn't stop for anyone and maybe that was the reason so many got left behind.

He knew Coach Green didn't believe him for a second, but he didn't push the subject. He laid a hand on his shoulder and looked him in the eye "I'm always here for you, Ace. Never forget that." And that was all he needed.

Practice was over. Ace and the rest of his teammates talked, while taking off their gear. "So, what's up with you and Amber, Ace? Still not talking?" Ace wasn't a fan of discussing his personal affairs with too many people, so he settled for shaking his head. Tatum placed his gear in his locker "Well, don't take it to heart. Amber's that way with everyone. I didn't think she would ever start dating, until you. She'll come around." He liked to believe she would, but he knew Amber and she was stubborn. It would take a long time to get back in her good graces.

Maddox grinned mischievously and leaned against the lockers "What about you, Josh?" He furrowed his eyebrows in confusion "What are you talking about?" He laughed "Don't act coy. Most of the school already knows about you and Bambi?" Tatum nodded "Yeah, I heard about that too, so how was it?" Josh went back to untying his laces and spoke, annoyed "How was what?"

"You know, being with Bambi. I hear she's awesome in bed."

Josh removed his cleats and placed them in his locker "And how would I know that?" Tatum rolled his eyes "Come on, we all heard the story. You complimented her today at lunch and she left with you after that." Josh's frown grew deeper "Where did you hear that?"

It was Maddox turn to look confuse "Madison. It's all over her website." Ace shook his head from his seat on the bench "Out of experience, I wouldn't believe anything Madison puts on that gossip website of hers. All she uses it for is too ruin people's reputations and relationships. It's disgusting."

Tatum nodded "Yeah, but she's still hot!" Him and Maddox high-fived on that. Josh's phone beeped and he pulled it out. He exhaled and stood up. "I got to go." They all knew what that meant. None of them spoke on it.

Ace got into his father's truck and prepared himself for the usual conversation they always had. "So, how did practice go?" *School was alright, thanks for asking.*

"Good. Scored a touchdown" His father hummed in response and tapped the steering wheel. "Coach Green told me about the scholarship withdrawal." Ace felt a headache coming on. "But, the scholarship was from Harlington, so it really doesn't matter. Still, I need you to focus Ace. We don't want to chance losing anymore offers. You have to take this serious. These are your dreams on the line."

By *your dreams*, Ace's father meant *his*. His father had almost went pro, but injured his knee. He was no longer allowed to play and his dreams faded along with his career. When he had found out he was having a son, he had been over the moon with joy. He now had someone to pass down his legacy to. In the beginning, Ace had enjoyed playing football. Making his father proud and spending time with him. Soon, the fun started turning into misery. They spent more time as player and coach and less time as father and son.

Ace had to miss out on a lot of childhood things, because of football. Football only left room for two things, school and *football*. If he had become interested in something other than that, his father would instantly shoot it down. Ace often wondered if his father even cared about what his dreams were. Probably not. He never asked. In his father's eyes they shared the same dreams. Ace wished his father would wake up.

Josh walked toward his father's office, greeting familiar faces. He knocked and was told to come in. His father held up a finger and walked around the office, as he talked into the phone.

"Sorry…I…No….I just can't make it….I'm sorry, but I'm sick with the flu….I swear, it….I'm in bed, right now," his father lied to whoever was on the phone, coughing for emphasis. His father told a few more lies and ended the call. He placed the phone down and adjusted his tie "Take my advice, son. Never date a Harlington woman. They're crazy I tell you."

Josh ignored his father's prejudice comment "You said you had something to discuss with me?" A grin took over his father's face and he nodded. He took a seat and motioned for Josh to do the same. His father clasped his hands together and leaned forward "For the past two weeks, I've been discussing you taking over the business with the staff. We've all decided you're ready to take over, so come this fall, I'm handing the business over to you." his father finished with a beaming smile. He thought the news would make Josh happy. It didn't.

"What about football?" Josh had planned on playing football his time in college, but now he wasn't even sure if he was going to attend college. How would he? Running the business was a stressful job. He couldn't possibly do that and attend college, while playing football.

His father frowned at his question and sat back in his chair "Well, you'll have to quit of course. You can't focus on that *and* running the business." Josh didn't respond. This wouldn't be the first time the business came before his happiness. There were many. He didn't have to question who his father loved more. All those days of being home alone or having no one to support him at his games. Josh didn't show how much it really hurt him, though. He smiled and laugh. Washing his sorrows away with drinks and parties. The happiness it gave him never lasted, though.

Josh's phone rang, breaking the tension filled silence. He knew who it was by the ringtone, so did his father. Not wanting to be taunted, he ignored the call. His father didn't let him get off that easy, though. "Carla, again?" he asked with a grin. Josh's jaw clenched for a moment and he nodded "Yes, and her name's *Courtney.*" His father stood up and began to walk toward his refrigerator.

"Carla, Courtney. It doesn't matter, they're all the same son. They only want us for our money and that's it. That's why you have to be careful. Don't go falling in love, because then they've trapped you and all your hard work would have been for nothing." He pulled out a bottle of liquor and grabbed two glasses "But, let's not discuss that right now. Today, is a day for celebration. In fact, I'm taking us to Sienna's tonight. Dinner on me."

Josh should have been happy of the fact that his father wanted to spend time with him. But, it was never out of genuine love and care. It always pertained to business. His father's ideas of father and son quality time consisted of company meetings and sharing a couple glasses of wine.

"I can't, I have homework." he lied. A habit he had picked up from his father. His father's eyes hardened for a moment, before he grinned "Forget about that. Pay some nerd to do it or ask Carla, you've got her wrapped around your finger." Josh didn't respond and only nodded. He didn't push it further. He didn't want a repeat of the last time he tried to go against his father's wishes. His stomach and sides were still sore.

His father lied to the doctor about what truly happened and he played along. Like father, like son. Just thinking about that night made his shoulder began to ache, again. To get rid of the painful thoughts, he downed the liquid in one gulp. His father slapped him on the shoulder "That a boy!" and proceeded to copy him.

The alcohol helped wash away his true thoughts and feelings. It didn't burn as it did the first time. Like his feelings, it was becoming less and less painful. He was becoming numb to it and he didn't care. The numbness filled him up, because the less he felt, the less he was hurt. He wondered when the day would come, when he would have no thoughts and feelings at all.

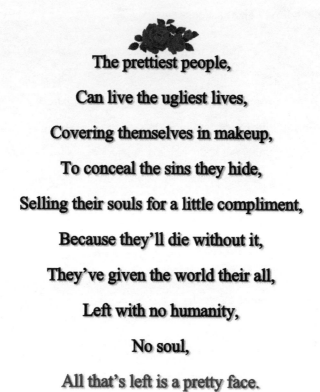

The prettiest people,

Can live the ugliest lives,

Covering themselves in makeup,

To conceal the sins they hide,

Selling their souls for a little compliment,

Because they'll die without it,

They've given the world their all,

Left with no humanity,

No soul,

All that's left is a pretty face.

CHAPTER FOUR

The Prettiest People

Courtney stared at the phone in anger, as it went to voicemail one again. "Ugh! Why won't he answer?!" she exclaimed. Amber looked up from her textbook and sighed "Maybe, he's busy Court." Courtney fell back against her bed and huffed "He's always busy. Doesn't he realize that I have feelings too?! I can't just keep sitting around waiting for him!" Amber shook her head and went back to studying for next week's test. Courtney suddenly set up and gasped "What if he's with another girl?!" Amber didn't respond, lost in her own mind.

Courtney crawled over to her and frowned "Seriously, Amber?! You're studying for a test that's probably not going to count." The other girl shrugged in response "You never know." Courtney rolled her eyes and pulled the book away from her paranoid best friend "Ugh, I need you to listen to me. I'm in a crises, right now! You're my best friend, you're supposed to help me!" Amber blew out a frustrated breath, knowing her friend wasn't going to let her study until she listened to her.

She turned to her, giving Courtney her full attention "Why would you think he's cheating on you?" Courtney frowned "The same reason you thought Ace was cheating on you…" she then grabbed her phone and typed something in. Amber had to squint her eyes when Courtney placed the bright phone to close too her face "…It's all over Gossip Guru." she whined.

Amber pushed the phone back a little to read it clearly. From what she could see, it was just Madison trying to stir up trouble, as usual. She placed the phone down and shook her head "Don't believe anything Madison puts on that stupid site of hers. It's all garbage. She's just trying to start drama, that's all."

Courtney scowled "No, I'm sure this is true. This is Bambi we're talking about, you know what type of girl she is." Courtney's arms crossed, as her scowl grew deeper. "Ugh, she's such a slut. Why does she flirt with *every* guy in school? I mean yes, she's pretty, but that doesn't mean you have to flaunt it."

Amber frowned. Courtney was starting to sound like Madison and all the other girls in school. She didn't see why everyone hated the girl so much. Yes, the girl was pretty, but a lot of girls were. So what she talked to guys, a lot of girls do. It was no secret that a lot of guys were interested in Bambi. Girls like to say it was only, because of her reputation, but that couldn't be true. A reputation wouldn't be able to keeps a boy's interest for that long. No matter how big it was.

"I think you're being too harsh, Court. I know there are a lot of rumors going on about Bambi, but I don't believe them. I mean honestly, when have you ever saw her even go up to a guy? Let alone flirt with one."

The times Amber would see Bambi, she would be sitting alone or keeping to herself. If she was talking to a guy, it was, because he initiated the conversation. Amber supposed it was a jealousy and insecurity thing that made girls so hateful. Often times, Amber felt bad for the girl, but she did nothing. It wasn't any of her problems. Plus, she was graduating soon. She didn't have time for any petty school drama.

Courtney processed it for a bit and was going to agree, but something wouldn't let her. She shook her head clear of thoughts "Come on, Amber. You're going to defend her?! Didn't she try flirting with Ace, once? I bet you she's the one he cheated on you with."

Amber stayed silent at this. She wanted to tell her best friend that she didn't really believe Ace had cheated on her, but she knew that would call for too much explanation and she didn't have the time for it.

Courtney must have took her silence for offence, because she quickly began to apologize. Amber waved her away "It's no big deal. Let's not talk about it." Courtney watched her for a minute "Do you miss him?" Amber looked away. Did she miss Ace? Of course she did, but they were two people with too many problems, that often got in the way of their relationship. Amber hadn't ended the relationship for just her, but him too. It was for the best.

"Yeah, I miss him. I miss him a lot" Courtney gave her best friend a sympathetic look. "Well, maybe you should trying giving him a chance to explain himself and hear his side of the story" Amber shook her head. She didn't need Ace to explain his side of the story, because she knew the truth.

Courtney was going to speak again, but her phone buzzed, interrupting her. She unlocked her phone and grinned. Amber's eyebrows knitted together "Who's that?" she asked, curiously. She leaned over to get a better look, but Courtney moved the phone away. "It's Tatum" Amber sat back and tilted her head "From the football team? What does he want?" Courtney sighed and played with her hair "Oh, nothing much. He just asked if I had any plans this weekend"

"And you said….."

Courtney's grin grew bigger "I said no" Amber closed her eyes and took a deep breath "Courtney, Josh and Tatum are really close" The other girl's eyebrow raised, nonchalantly "And?"

"And, if you start dating Tatum that could not only damage their friendship, but you and Josh's relationship, as well." Courtney waved her away. She thought Amber was being paranoid. Josh was probably somewhere having fun, so why couldn't she?

"Relax, Amber. It's not like we're going to be doing anything scandalous. We're just going to hangout. Nothing more."

Amber shook her head in disapproval "I still don't think you should do this, Court. Friendly or not. How do you think Josh is going to feel?" Courtney rolled her eyes

"Ugh….you're such a mom. Nothing bad is going to happen. What Josh doesn't know won't hurt him"

Courtney giggled as she read Tatum's text. She received another text, as she was going to reply. She opened it and couldn't help that her stomach fluttered a bit.

Hey, Sorry for ignoring you. Was @ the office. U busy?

Tatum, now forgotten, she quickly responded to Josh's text.

It's fine. Not doin anything. Y?

We should hangout. U free 2nite?

Yeah. U can pick me up @10

Alright. Try not to get caught this time.

Shut up! Lol.

Courtney tried not to act so giddy, as she searched for an outfit. She picked out a crop top and her beach shorts from the previous summer. She would be cold, but it would be worth it. Josh wouldn't be able to take his eyes off her. He said he wanted to spend some time together. She hoped that meant they could finally do something that didn't involve clothes being shed.

Courtney spotted Josh's car and quickly ran across the street, toward it. She opened the car's door and got inside. "Hey," she greeted and leaned over to kiss his cheek. He gave her a small smile, which she could tell was forced. She ignored it, not wanting to make him upset.

She waited for him to comment her on her outfit, but he didn't "So, where are we going? Maybe, we could go to *The Warehouse*. I think I heard someone say the *Pirates* were going to be there. It'll be fun." she gushed, trying to lighten the mood.

Josh reached over to grab her hand. Courtney's stomach fluttered and she smiled at his rare display of affection. He gave her quick peck on the lips "Actually, I was thinking we could just spend some time alone with each other. Just the two of us." he whispered, suggestively.

Josh's leaned in to kiss her, again, but she turned her head away. He frowned "What's wrong?" She shrugged "All we ever do is *do it*, whenever you're hurting or upset. Why don't you try talking about it? Maybe, it'll make you feel better." she said and placed her hand to his cheek.

Josh retracted away from her and sat back against the seat. His face was emotionless, as he spoke, but the frustration in his voice was obvious "I'm not upset and I'm not hurt. I wanted us to spend some time together, but it's clear that you're not up for it."

He reached to start the ignition. Courtney bit her lip in thought. This wasn't how she expected things to go. She wanted to spend time with him and she wanted this time to be different. Not like all the others, that involved mostly touching and less talking. The scowl on his face let her know today that wouldn't happen.

The car cranked and she grabbed his face, pulling it to hers. She tried to put all her feelings into the kiss. When their lips separated, she looked into his eyes, hoping they would mirror her own. The disappointment was scorching, but she pushed it away. Along with, the sadness in her heart. As, the kiss got more intense, she pretended the flutters were still there. *I'll just have to try harder next time. I want this.* **He loves me**. That is what she told herself.

The night sky help conceal her tears. *He loves me.* He had to. She was always the person he came to, when he was upset. She was always the person to comfort him. *He loved her,* is what she told herself. But, as days passed, it was getting harder and harder to convince herself of that.

He removed her top and she felt as cold on the outside as she did inside. She wanted to wrap her arms around herself, but knew she would look foolish acting modest. She didn't want him threatening her with leaving, again. His lips were on hers, but she felt nothing this time. She closed her eyes and tried to focus on something else, other than her discomfort. *It's okay, he loves me.*

Madison stood in front of the mirror and struck another pose. She pulled her shirt down a little to show a bit more cleavage. She snapped the picture and posted it. Comments came rolling in.

She read them with satisfaction. They made her feel good. She wasn't one of those girls that hid from the spotlight. She relished in it. There were times when other girls tried to steal it from her. Girls like Bambi, but she always put a stop to that. The spotlight would always find its way back to her. Like, now. She was sure no one was thinking of Bambi, as they liked and complimented her pictures. Bambi was no competition to her and she still wondered why so many guys fawned after her. She dressed, as if she was still fourteen, she was boring.

Madison held her phone up to take another picture, this time without her shirt. Abruptly, her bedroom door was slammed opened. Her mother walked into the room with a frown. Her eyes fell on Madison and her frown grew deeper. She took long strides toward her and snatched the phone away from her. Before Madison could react, her mother's hand reached up to smack her. "Just look at you. Posing and taking pictures like a slut. I get home and the kitchen's a mess! Go clean it!" Madison didn't move. Her mother placed her hands on her hips "Didn't you hear me?! Go clean that kitchen, now!"

Madison hurried out of the room. She walked into the kitchen and dread washed over her. Frank stood up straight and closed the refrigerator. With a beer in his hand he walked over to her. "It's kind of cold in here, you might want to put on some clothes…." His finger ran across her shoulder "…But, I'm not complaining."

"Get your hands off of me!" Madison pulled away from him, just as her mother walked into the kitchen. She looked between the two of them "What's going on in here?" Frank took a sip from the beer "Nothing. I just asked Madison on her plans after she graduates." Her mother rolled her eyes and scoffed "Please, she doesn't have any plans. The only job she'll ever be able to get is at a drive thru or corner." Madison tried not to let the sting of her mother's words get to her. Discreetly, Frank let his eyes roam over Madison, again. Her mother saw this, but pretended she didn't. Out of anger and jealously, she grabbed her daughter's arm and shoved her "Go put on some clothes! Can't you see we have company?!" Frank made sure Madison's mother wasn't looking and gave her a wink. Madison rushed out of the kitchen, holding in her tears.

Cupping the water from the faucet, she splashed it onto her face. She looked into the mirror and grimaced. A handprint from her mother's slap had been left on her face. She touched it and winced. Yet another bruise she was going to have to conceal. Madison hated wearing the makeup, but it was like her armor. Underneath it, she was just as vulnerable as the people she bullied. Years of wearing the makeup had now made her skin dry and covered in marks. She looked way beyond the years of her actual age.

Her phone buzzed. Someone else had liked her pictures. This time she didn't feel happy. She felt empty and numb. The comments now meant nothing and weren't going to help her. People expected her to have the perfect life by the façade she displayed, but her life was far from perfect.

"Madison! Kitchen, now!"

She cleared her throat and tried to make her voice sound normal. "I'm coming!" It didn't matter. Her mother wouldn't notice the difference anyway. Her phone buzzed again, but this time she turned it off. She opened her drawer and sighed. The blade glinted in the bathroom's light. It called out to her. Gave her promises of taking the pain away and she trusted it. This would never fail her. This was always there when she needed it. She picked it up and smiled sadly "I was hoping I wouldn't need you, today." She didn't feel the pain. Like everything else, she was numb to it.

We all know we're going to die at one point,

And we know there's no way to predict it,

Everyone's death is different,

But there's one thing that sets each death apart,

Some deaths seem more important than others,

So you see,

Dying is not the scary part,

The scariest part is figuring out no one will notice.

CHAPTER FIVE

Never Noticed

"Bambi"

She paused in her steps and looked over her shoulder. Courtney stalked over to the girl and crossed her arms "I have to talk to you" Bambi gave a short and slow nod. Together, she and Courtney walked over to the nearby lockers for privacy. That still didn't stop some students from trying to eavesdrop on their conversation.

Bambi's heart pounded against her chest, as she followed Courtney to the lockers. She didn't know what she wanted, but she was sure it couldn't be anything good. They made it to the lockers and Courtney stared at her with a scowl. She tried to remember if she had done anything to make the other girl mad, but couldn't come up with anything.

Courtney looked her over, before rolling her eyes "I heard about you and Josh." Bambi wanted to scream. Because of yesterday's incident with Josh, people now thought she and him had something going on. Madison hadn't hesitated in mixing up the truth about what really happened and posting it on her blog.

Bambi shook her head "You've got the wrong idea. Josh and I-" Courtney held a hand up, cutting her off. "You don't have to lie to me," Her scowl turned into a glare "Look, I don't care about you having a little crush on Josh. Lots of girls do, but try to keep it at that. Josh is mine and I'm not going to let some slut like you try to seduce him. So, back off!" Having spoken her mind, Courtney left.

Bambi's eyes watered and she clenched her fist. All the things people said and believed about her were false. She wanted to tell everyone this. To yell and let out all of her pains and frustrations on them, but she didn't. The sound of heels clicking made her look up. *Why am I not surprised?*

Madison strutted up to her and grimaced "I saw what just happened. And I have to say, for once, I kind of feel bad for you," A surprised expression took over Bambi's face. Madison was acting sympathetic to her? *That doesn't make sense.* Madison's grimace was replaced by a smirk "But, maybe this will teach you to not flirt with other girl's boyfriends." The cheerleader gave her wink and walked away. *Now, that made sense.*

Bambi inhaled and exhaled, letting her shoulders rise and fall. It was a calming method her mother had taught her. *It's okay, I'm fine.* She ignored what had just happened and thought of the future. All night, she had stayed up preparing the lunches. She wanted them to be perfect. She was excited to finally have a friend. Earlier, she had tried looking for him, but couldn't find him. She would just have to push her anxiousness down, until lunch.

"All students report to the school's auditorium, I repeat all students report to the school's auditorium."

Bambi was happy to exit the classroom and get away from the glares Courtney was giving her. She held her head down, as she walked toward the auditorium along with the other students. A hand fell on her shoulder and she jumped a little, startled. Josh gave her an apologetic smile. He pulled his hand away to rub the back of his neck "Hey, Bambi. Could I talk to you for a moment?" Other students watched them, whispering to one another.

"I don't think that would be a good idea." She turned around to leave, but he grabbed her arm gently, stopping her. "Please. Just for a moment. It'll be quick, I promise." She gave a short nod and pulled her arm free. They walked alongside each other, as they spoke.

"I want to apologize for yesterday. I didn't mean anything by it and I wasn't apart of Madison putting it on her blog."

She glanced at him out of the corner of her eye "Thank you. I'm glad you don't believe any of that stuff."

They had made it to the auditorium. Josh stopped and turned to her "I would like to get to know you better. The real, Bambi. If that's okay with you."

Bambi could see the sincerity in his eyes. She wanted to be hopeful. She wanted to give him a chance, but she knew she couldn't. He seemed like a nice guy, but he would just make her life more complicated then what it already was. Her eyes wondered around the cluster of students, hoping no one was watching them. Not too far away, both Courtney and Madison observed them. One wearing a scowl and the other a smirk.

Bambi felt her stomach drop. She turned back to Josh, who was awaiting a reply. His smile made her answer even more difficult. "I'm sorry," his smile dropped "We can't be friends. It'll cause too much trouble. Thank you for the offer, though. Goodbye." she rushed away. Josh looked around, locking eyes with Courtney. His frown made her look away.

Bambi sat towards the back. This way she could see without being seen. On stage were two police officers and the principal, they all wore gloomy expressions, along with a few teachers. A body sat next to hers. She glanced at the person for a second, before looking away quickly, realizing who it was. She acted normal around the boy dressed in all black, even though he scared her.

"Thanks for saving me a seat."

Bambi could recognize that voice anywhere. The girl shook her head vigorously "N-No need to thank me." she stuttered, moving her bag out of the seat. Madison and the rest of her friends sat down. She smiled at the girl, then twisted around and smirked "Hey, Bambi. We just keep bumping into each other." Bambi didn't respond to the girl's taunting words and faced forward. "Hey, I'm talking-"

"Quiet! Everyone, quiet!"

The principal spoke into the microphone. All conversation ceased. Everyone's attention was now on the stage.

"I know you all are wondering why we called you out of your classes so suddenly. Well, I bring grave news."

he paused for a moment "Today, we were informed of the loss of one of our students." Everyone waited for him to continue. It seemed to pain the principal to speak of it. Bambi wondered if he knew the student well. "Last night, one of our students-Peyton Smith hung himself. He was found this morning by his mother."

A picture of the boy appeared on the projector's screen. Bambi's heart dropped. This couldn't be true. It had to be some kind of joke. One of the police officers went onto speaking on how bullying is wrong and a serious offence. Bambi tuned them out. *He was gone?* But, how? She had just saw him, yesterday. He seemed upset, but she didn't think he would kill himself. Maybe, they weren't alike. He probably had it worse. Her eyes watered and she bit her trembling lips. *Why did he have to die?*

Students began to whispers amongst themselves. Including the bullies themselves that sat in front of Bambi.

"Who was he?"

"I never saw him. Are they sure he was a student here?"

"Wait! I think I know who he was. He was that nerd some of the guys on the football teamed bullied and called gay. It was just a joke, though. I don't understand why he would kill himself over something like that. I mean come on, man up."

Madison shook her head and sighed *"I know, but it's still sad though. Some people just take bullying too far."*

Bambi wanted to reach up and hit Madison for her stupid, hypocritical words. She said some people took bullying too far, but she was one of those people. She was just too vain to see it.

Of course they wouldn't understand. They were the bullies themselves. They didn't know how it felt to be put down and ridiculed. They were the ones who liked to belittle people to make themselves feel superior. *Why was it no one else could see that? Why did people like to make bullying cool?* Even some of the teachers laughed along to the taunts and encouraged them, others just watched not offering an ounce of their help.

"Did you know him?"

Bambi was pulled out of her thoughts and turned to the boy dressed in all black. He watched her curiously. He could tell the news about the boy's death had hurt her by the distressed look on her face. She looked away from him and shook her head. "No. I never got the chance to." And now, she never would.

A grudge is like a cage,

It traps you,

Keeping you away from all the great prospects of life,

The days will keep passing by until you'll finally find yourself alone,

But, if you choose to let that grudge go you'll see,

A little forgiveness will open that cage and set you free.

CHAPTER SIX

Grudges

Unlike yesterday, the sun was out. It shined down, despite yesterday's previous dark news. Bambi had been depressed many times before, but today beat all others. Peyton had been both lost and found in a matter of a few hours. The first and last time she had saw him, he had been nothing, but kind and generous. He didn't deserve death, but then again, no one did. Death was something uncontrollable and unpredictable. It often snuck up on most or maybe they were oblivious to it the whole time.

A few teachers had spoken about the boy-who she now knew as Peyton. They didn't say much, only the basics. He was a quiet boy, didn't cause much trouble, and got decent grades. Bambi wondered how long it would take, until his death was replaced by something else. A sports ad or new, exciting gossip. Bambi didn't know the boy well, but she was sure he had been feeling the way she felt most days.

She couldn't define the feeling, but she supposed the word 'heavy' would do. The feeling was uncomfortable and unwanted, but she still carried it around. It's not like she wanted to, she had no control of when it came or left. When this feeling came around there was no sun, only the shadows that tried to consume her and every ounce of contentment she had. Her thread was thin and fragile, and sometimes the weight was too heavy to hold. Still, she always made sure there was something there that kept the thread from breaking. Peyton's thread had broken, releasing the weight on him. Before, he could process what had happened the weight had come crashing down. It held him down, making it hard for him to breathe. He might have called for help, might have even screamed too. No one had heard his cries for help, though. It was too late. Slowly and silently, the weight grew heavier and heavier, until he was no longer crying. Until, he was no longer breathing.

The car stopped and Bambi looked out the car's window, seeing they had finally arrived. She sighed and opened the door to step out, but her mother's voice stopped her. "Are you sure you want to go, today?

I'm sure Ms. Clover will understand-" Releasing a frustrated breath, Bambi spoke "I'm fine mom." Her mother's face fell, her hand moving to rub Bambi's back. "Is everything alright, sweetheart? You've been down since you got home from school yesterday. Did something happen-"

Angrily, Bambi snatched away from her mother "I said I'm fine, mom! Just stop!" Her mother bit her lip, sadly and pulled her hand away. "Okay, I'm sorry sweetheart. I'm just worried about you, if you…" Bambi's face fell into her usual emotionless mask when her mother would try to get her to express her feelings. She opened the car's door and stuck her foot out "I have to go mom, see you later." Her mother paused in what she had been saying. With a sigh, her head fell, but then she lifted it with a smile on her face "Okay, dear. See you later, love you." Bambi stepped out of the car, muttering "I love you, too."

Old Man Jones looked at the teens in front of him and knew he had his work cut out for him. Clapping his hands he began giving out orders "Okay, Ms. Clover tells me y'all are here for missing community service hours. Well, I found that downright disgraceful! So, here's what we're going to do. You guys are going to do what I say and hopefully we'll never have to see each other, again. Got it!"

They nodded. Old Man Jones didn't like their response and yelled louder, this time "I said, got it!" They all opened their mouths to reply this time. "That's better," Old Man Jones placed his hands on his hips, trying to decipher what he was going to have each teen do. "You, there." He said, pointing to Bambi. She instantly straightened up and he chuckled "I have a list with a few things I need on it. You and muscles over there will go get them,"

His eyes shifted to Madison, she smirked. Old Man Jones inwardly sighed. She was going to be his toughest one to crack. "You and pretty boy will be running a couple errands for me," Madison's smirk dropped and she frowned. Lastly, his eyes fell on Amber and Courtney "You two will be working with me." Madison crossed her arms. She didn't find it fair that the two best friends were paired up.

Old Man Jones looked the teens over, once again. He sighed and shook his head at their emotionless faces.

Bambi and Ace had finished getting everything off of Old Man Jones' list. They were now waiting on Madison and Josh, who had taken the truck to run errands. The sun shined brightly, today. Giving the town a look of peace and happiness. It was a lie. Many of the people who walked throughout the town, wearing smiles on their face were the most miserable. Their smiles were like masks to their pain. Bambi would know, she was just like them.

It was getting hot and Bambi was beginning to get annoyed by the heat. The boy used his arm to wipe at his forehead and turned to her "Want to sit?" he asked and nodded toward a bench. The sight of the empty bench in the shade relieved Bambi. She quickly nodded her head and made her way over toward it.

They sat. After a while, Bambi's stomach began to growl. She remembered the lunch her mother had made her bring and took it out. Her hand froze when she saw the second sandwich. She figured her mother must have just placed her lunch bag in the refrigerator. Saving them, instead of throwing them away. Taking a deep breath and swallowing her sadness, she placed the second sandwich back inside the bag.

Peyton's death had caused a huge impact on her. But, when she thought of throwing the lunches away, Peyton's words had stopped her. They reminded her that going without eating is really dangerous and even deadly. It made her wonder if anyone would grieve this much at *her* death. Especially someone she barely knew. At times it didn't seem like it. She felt alone in her pains and sufferings. It felt like no one was there.

The boy's stomach growled, grabbing both of their attentions. Sitting up, Ace groaned and rubbed his stomach.

Bambi's eyes shifted to her lunch bag, which held the second sandwich. The sandwich had been made with the hopes of starting a friendship with the person she was giving it to. "Here." The boy's eyebrows were furrowed as he looked from her to the sandwich. He took it and held it in his hands. Bambi watched him. *Maybe, he was experiencing the same emotions I had.* The boy sniffed it "What did you do to it?" *He had not.* Bambi scowled and glared at the boy "Nothing" He gave a soft chuckled and held it in the air carelessly "Yeah, sure. If nothing was wrong with it, why would you give it to me?" *Why couldn't he just be grateful?* "It was for my friend." He smirked "Then why didn't you give it to your *friend*?"

Bambi shut her eyes and took a deep breath. *Hold it in.* "I didn't get the chance to." He didn't let up on her "And, why is that?" Her voice wavered a little and she could tell he heard it to. He probably thought that meant she was lying. "Because, I can't."

"And, why can't you?"

"Because,"

Hold it in. It's okay. Bambi could feel her emotions getting the best of her. She was trying to keep them in, but it was becoming hard. It was obvious the boy didn't know how much his words were hurting her. She hoped he didn't say anything else and just accepted the sandwich.

"Because, what?"

Forgetting all attempt of self-control, Bambi broke. They were all the same. None of them cared. They took everything as a joke. Someone had just lost their life. Someone they wouldn't remember or worry about. They didn't understand what it felt like to feel so alone in a room full of people. And, yet they got to live their lives care free. It wasn't fair.

"Because, he's dead!"

All humor disappeared from Ace's face, as he gazed up at the distressed girl. He had been joking with Bambi, but it was obvious she hadn't found anything funny. Her words still rang in his ears. *Her friend was dead?* That had to mean she was friends with the boy who had committed suicide, but they didn't seem like the ideal friends. Maddox and Tatum

75

had been a part of the bullying. They didn't seem to care that the boy had committed suicide, because of it. Their lives went on as normal.

Rage was clear in Bambi's eyes as she stared down at him. "He's dead, okay?! You and your stupid friends killed him! You guys probably thought he could take it, because he didn't fight back, right?! Well, he couldn't! It got too much for him and he broke! What did he ever do to you?!"

Ace's surprised expression melted into a frown. He hadn't been a part of the bullying. He never said or did anything! Maybe that was the problem. Ace couldn't put all the blame on his friends, though. Numerous of times, he had observed the boy being bullied by his friends, but as usual he did nothing about it. Now, he regretted that he hadn't.

Bambi gave one final shake of her head and turned to walk away. Abruptly, Ace's hand shot out to grab hers. "Wait! I'm sorry." Slowly, Bambi looked from their joined hands to his eyes. They stayed like that for a moment. Staring at each other. Bambi then shook her head, vigorously and pulled her hand free from his. "I'm not the one you should be apologizing to, but it's too late for that, now."

Ace frowned and released a breath "What my friends did was wrong, but I had nothing to do with it." Bambi's frown turned into a glare "You had nothing to do with it?! Sure, you might not have said or done anything to him, but you still watched and did nothing. Doing nothing is just as bad as doing something."

He took in her words and stood up, placing the sandwich on the bench "And what about you?" Bambi's eyebrows furrowed "What about me?" He took a step closer toward her, she took one back. He walked until her back was against a nearby tree. She was trapped. Ace leaned until their faces were inches apart "You're hear preaching to me about criticizing and judging people when you're doing the same thing." She scowled "It's not the same. You-" He interrupted her "And how isn't it the same? Am I not a person just like you? Do I not have feelings? What? Because, I'm *popular* I shouldn't feel."

Bambi opened her mouth to speak, but closed it and settled for glaring at him. Seeing he had rendered her speechless, he stepped away from her. "There's no good or bad people. We're just humans who sometimes do good or bad stuff. The sooner you accept that the calmer you'll be."

Bambi rolled her eyes and crossed her arms. Ace stared at her for a moment and then, held his hand out. "Look it's clear we both made a misconception, so how about a truce." Her eyes looked at his opened hand and she scoffed. She shouldered passed him and sat back in her original spot. He followed her, making her scoot over to put more distance between them.

Ace frowned and picked up his sandwich. "You know? You're meaner than you look." She gave him a sarcastic smile, taking a bite out of her sandwich. Ace shrugged and unwrapped the sandwich. He took a bite and made a sound of approval. The sandwich was finished in three bites. Three huge bites.

Bambi stared at him in disbelief. He burped and rubbed his stomach "That was good. I forgot how important lunch was." Reaching into her bag, she pulled out the extra water bottle she had and handed it to him. He thanked her and downed the water in big gulps. Bambi watched him and tilted her head "Is this a habit of yours?" He placed the bottled down and raised an eyebrow "Hmm?"

She nodded toward the sandwich wrapper "Not eating lunch. You said you forgot how important it was." He looked back at the field "Somethings are more important than lunch." Bambi's eyebrows knitted together "There's nothing more important than your health." She knew that was very hypocritical of her to say, but she had grown accustomed to not eating and so did her body. The boy turned to her and grinned. She could tell it was fake "I don't know. You tell me. Is football more important than my health?"

Bambi chewed the inside of her cheek in thought "I hope it's not." He chuckled and shook his head Truthfully, Bambi didn't know why she was being this open with him. Usually, she wasn't even able to form a sentence when talking to a boy, yet alone hold a conversation.

"But, at least you call it how it is. I suck." Bambi felt bad, then. She decided to say something to hopefully cheer him up. "Well, I'm sure with practice you'll get better. You might even become a quarterback one day."

The boy's chuckle was softer, this time. He sat back against the bleachers "I am the quarterback."

Bambi grimaced and scolded herself. She really need to work on her people skills.

"It's fine" Bambi's head snapped in his direction

"What?"

"It's fine. What you said hadn't upset me." She nodded and fidgeted with her fingers. They sat in a comfortable silence.

Bambi glanced at the boy out of the corner of her eye. He was starting to make her uncomfortable. Having enough of it, she spoke "Please, stop." He grinned at her "You're interesting." Her cheeks flushed and she quickly, changed the subject "F-Football." He frowned, nor sure what she meant by that.

"You said it was more important than your health. Why do you think that?" He shook his head "I didn't say that. I meant some think that football are more important than one's health. And others are just too tired to try and tell them differently." An unusual emotion flashed in his eyes, but Bambi didn't address it.

"What's your name?" He looked taken back by her odd and unexpected question. Looking her over, he sighed and leaned to rest his elbows on his knees "You really don't know who I am?" She looked to the sky and thought about it. Once she got her conclusion, she shook her head with a smile "Nope, not a clue." He chuckled "Ace." She placed a finger to her lip "Hmm…Ace?" Her eyes scanned him and she nodded "Sounds fitting. My name's Bambi. I apologize for being mean to you, earlier."

He raised an eyebrow at her bipolar behavior. He also didn't mention that he already knew who she was and nodded his head.

Both of them didn't speak, after that. Occasionally, Ace would sneak glances at her. Bambi's sat consumed in her thoughts. Tomorrow, she wouldn't fail on her task. At least, that was what she hoped. Ace probably thought she was weird, suddenly asking him for his name. But, after Peyton's death, she had made a vow. She would make sure to never meet someone and not get their name. You never know; tomorrow could be someone's last day.

Their work for today was over, they were now waiting for their rides. The farm's volunteer programed required that students were picked up and dropped off only by their parents.

Madison had left the group seconds ago, claiming she had to use the bathroom. She walked through the old house. Her hand was held over her nose, blocking the smell of it. She screwed up her face at all the tacky decorations and antique furniture. "Farm people." she muttered, with a roll of her eyes.

It didn't take her long to find the bathroom. She stepped inside and pulled out her phone. The phone rang twice, before it was answered.

"Ugh! Why haven't you called me?"

Madison laughed "Relax. You know why I haven't called, I told you Ms. Clover put me in this stupid volunteer program for my community service hours."

Tiffany huffed through the phone *"Still, I've been bored all day. There's literally nothing to do in this town."*

The corners of Madison mouth quirked up into a smirk. "I think I have something that my change that," Quickly, Madison opened the bathroom's door and stuck her head out. She made sure no one was around, before she continued to speak.

"I've got some more gossip." This seemed to make Tiffany perk up.

"Really, who?"

"Our favorite. Sweet, little Bambi" Tiffany's excitement died down. She gave a meek reply

"Oh,"

Madison's forehead creased "Oh? What do you mean, oh? Aren't you excited to hear what it is?"

Tiffany sighed through the phone *"Yes, I admit it was fun to mess with Bambi in the beginning, but now it's just getting boring. Most of the stuff we put on the website about her is mostly made up, anyways,"*

"And?"

"And, I want real gossip, Madison. Not just made up stories about Bambi. Plus, don't you think this has gone on long enough? We've been at her since freshmen year. I think she's had enough."

Madison listened to Tiffany's words and instantly became upset "I'll decide when she's had enough. Until, then she's going to continue to get what she deserves,"

The line had gone silent. Madison thought Tiffany had hung up until she spoke

"What happened?"

Madison didn't know what she referring to and asked her to clarify.

"What happened between you and Bambi? Why do you hate her so much?" Madison froze. No one had really attempted to ask her where the source of her hate for Bambi came from. Sometimes she didn't even know herself why her hate for the girl was so strong.

Shaking her head clear of thoughts, she spoke. "It doesn't matter what happened. All that matters is that it did happen and I'm making sure she doesn't get away with it,"

Well, whatever happened, happened years ago, Madison. Can't you let it go?

That was something Madison had thought about often. Could she let her hate for Bambi go? Part of her disagreed completely, Bambi was getting what she deserved. But, a small part of her. A part of herself, she hadn't seen in years. The part of herself, she had abandoned, told her what she was doing was wrong. That part of herself remembered the days, before the incident.

"I have to go."

Madison hung up the phone and looked into the mirror. Painful memories had begun to surface. Her face expressed everything she was feeling. Anger, frustration, hate and one that she kept to herself. Pain. Tiffany didn't know what she was talking about. She was clueless like everyone. Bambi wasn't a saint.

She had done things too. Some said it was foolish to hold a grudge, but Madison saw it as her encouragement. It's what kept her going. Sure, what happened had been years ago, but Madison wasn't going to let Bambi get away with it. She wasn't going to forget or allow Bambi to, until the girl felt everything she had felt during that time.

Madison took the time to fix her appearance. She checked it once more in the mirror, before becoming satisfied. She stepped out of the bathroom, bumping into Old Man Jones. Not expecting him, she fumbled and stuttered out a reply. "Y-Yes."

"Gossiping leads to bad, bad things. Heed my words. You might want to back out of all that now, while you still can." Old Man Jones let that be his final words, before moving pass her into the bathroom.

Madison stared out in a daze for a moment, as Old Man Jones' words rang throughout her mind. She knew she shouldn't have paid his words any attention. He was just an old man. What did he know? But, his words had an edge to them. Not liking how frazzled his words had made her, she shook them off. The man was obviously out of his mind. It was just a little gossip. What's the worst that could happen? Later, she would regret not listening to Old Man Jones' words.

Courtney's blood boiled, after eavesdropping on Madison's and Tiffany's conversation. She had been waiting to use the restroom and heard everything. Madison was worse than she thought. The girl was downright evil! Hearing footsteps, she had quickly hid around the corner not to be caught. Courtney knew Madison wasn't going to pay Old Man Jones' words any mind. She was too far gone and didn't see anything wrong with what she was doing. She felt stupid for all the times she had believed the stuff Madison had posted on her blog. She also wanted to know what had happened between Madison and Bambi. She truly hated the girl.

Courtney now felt guilty for confronting Bambi, without knowing the whole story. She had got caught up in the drama, it was just too believable or maybe it was just too distracting. The students in RoseOak didn't care whether the gossip spread was true or not. It was their entertainment. They enjoyed the few days of someone's self-esteem being destroyed, because it built up theirs. It made their lives seem a little less miserable. Courtney knew she had to tell Amber about what she had just heard. She didn't want her friend to be blinded and deceived as she had been.

Courtney spotted Amber still leaned against the farm's fences. A tense expression was on her friend's face. She noticed the cause of it. Ace was standing a couple feet away from her, occasionally glancing her way. He would look away when Amber met his eyes. Which only led to her staring at him for a while, emotions passing through her eyes. Courtney rolled her eyes. They were so annoying *and* oblivious. *Just get back together, already.* Courtney scurried over to her friend and looked around them, before whisper-ring "You won't believe what I just heard," Amber looked up with a scowl "Not right now, Court. I have a headache from all those orders Old Man Jones had us make." she said, and massaged the back of her neck.

Courtney frowned "This is important." she didn't speak in a whisper this time. Amber sighed and crossed her arms. She ran both hands through her hair. She then crossed her arms, giving Courtney her full attention. "Fine. I'm listening." Courtney then proceeded to relay the conversation between Madison and Tiffany.

Amber listened to her best friend and couldn't understand why she was so upset. Sure, it was annoying that Madison deceived so many people with the rumors she spread, but it wasn't something worth getting distraught over. They more than likely weren't going to ever see Madison, after high school. There had been many girls like Madison in the past and there would be more in the future. Their goal was to make others feel bad in order to make themselves feel accepted and wanted.

After high school, they would most likely be nobodies as sad as that was, but it was the truth. Girls like Madison spent too much of their time trying to ruin others' lives that they never saw how damaged theirs were. When they did finally realize, it would be too late and they would be alone. Because, without insignificant high school popularity, they were nothing.

Courtney finished her rant with a huff. Amber shrugged "Okay, I get what you're trying to say, but I don't understand why you're so mad," Courtney looked at her in disbelief "What do you mean you don't understand? She deceived me Amber. She played me like a fool." Amber shook her head "Are you mad, because she deceived you or are you mad, because you believed her?" Courtney crossed her arms and leaned against the fence with a shrug "I don't know. Both, I guess."

Amber nodded and pulled out her buzzing phone. "Our feelings can be our downfall. The year's almost over, we're not going to see half of these people ever again in our lives. Madison included. Nothing they say should change or effect you in any way."

Courtney pouted "How am I supposed to do that? Their words really hurt, Amber." she spoke in a whine. Amber turned the next page in her textbook "Just think of it this way, every time a person insults you they're just expressing how they truly feel inside." Courtney's eyebrows knitted together. She tried to think it over, but then shook her head, becoming confused. "But that doesn't make sense." Amber shrugged "Human feelings have never made sense. Especially the feelings of teenage girls."

Courtney sighed. Her conscious was eating her up "I still feel bad for the way I treated Bambi, though. She even tried to explain what happened, but I didn't listen." Amber paused and looked up at her friend, raising an eyebrow "Why didn't you. All that could have been avoided, you know?" Courtney ran a hand down her face "I know that, but I guess a part of me was jealous that Josh was showing her attention. I can barely get him to acknowledge me at school."

Amber gave her friend a pointed look "Courtney we've talked about this, before. When it comes to Josh you seem to lose all senses and do stuff recklessly, it's not healthy. If you're not careful you might get in real trouble next time." Courtney waved her off "Okay, Okay. Enough about me. We're talking about Bambi, right now."

Amber rolled her eyes. Her friend always asked for her advice, but never wanted to hear the truth. It was exhausting.

Amber began texting someone "What's there to talk about?" Courtney groaned, letting her head fall back. "I feel bad for what I did." Amber shrugged "Then apologize."

Courtney looked to the sky and hummed "I'll think about it, but part of me wonders why Madison always goes to great lengths to hurt the girl. She said Bambi had done something to her in the past. What do you think?" Amber sat up and took in a deep inhale, beginning to pack up her stuff. "I don't understand the relationship between Madison and Bambi. They're both so different. But, there is one similar thing I notice about the two of them, every time I see them." Courtney tilted her head "What?"

"They both seem lonely."

Courtney let those words sit with her. She snapped out of her thoughts, once Amber sat up off the fence. A sulking expression took over her face "Where are you going?" Amber grabbed her bag off the ground and pointed "I have to go. My dad's here." Courtney tried not to grimace. Amber's dad had always scared her and it wasn't a secret he didn't like her. She had caught him once telling Mrs. Hart she wasn't a good influence on Amber. It satisfied her that Amber hadn't listened to him and continued to be her friend.

Courtney glowered "Fine. But, we have to do something this weekend. We haven't hung out in *forever.*" Amber rolled her eyes at her friend's exaggeration, but agreed. She made sure not to make eye contact with Ace, as she made her way towards her father's car.

Not long after Amber's departure, did Ace's father come for him. It was now just her, Josh, Bambi, and Madison.

Courtney contemplated if she should go and speak to the girl. Coming to a decision, she made her way over to the other girl. Josh and Madison watched on, curiously. Bambi was in her own world, as she read her book she had recently got. She didn't notice Courtney come up behind her, so when the other girl spoke, she dropped the book she was holding.

She stared at the girl startled, hoping she wasn't here to start a fight with her over the rumors Madison had spread. Courtney raised an eyebrow, before shaking her head and squatting down to pick up the book. Bambi watched her in shock, but then began to help her. They stood up and Courtney handed her the books "Sorry," Bambi accepted the books and shook her head "It's okay."

Courtney looked around and cleared her throat "Um….I just want to apologize-for earlier. I shouldn't have attacked you like that without your explanation first," Bambi was too flabbergasted by the girl's apology to speak. Courtney continued to speak "I'm sorry for judging you like everyone else, but now that we've cleared things out maybe we can be friend-"

Bambi cut her off. She tilted her head and her eyebrows wrinkled together. "You want to be my friend?" she asked in disbelief. Courtney nodded, giving her a friendly smile "Yeah" Bambi let her eyes glance around the farm, before they fell back on the girl in front of her "Why?" Courtney looked taken back and Bambi explained herself "It's just weird. Yesterday, you hated and even threatened me. I'm not trying to be mean, just curious."

Courtney nodded and then began to explain the conversation between Madison and Tiffany, along with her feelings on it.

Bambi listened to the other girl explain herself and now understood what the problem was. "You don't have to be my friend, because you feel guilty. What happened was in the past. I'm not going to hold it against you" Courtney shook her head "No. It's not just that. I do feel guilty, but I also want to be your friend. Not out of guilt or anything."

Bambi could not understand why Courtney was having such a change of heart. She recalled many times when Courtney and other girls would judge her based on the rumors Madison spread. Part of Bambi wanted to believe the girl was being genuine, but another part of her was worried about being deceived. It had been done many times before and they all started the same way. *I want to be your friend.* What they really meant was, *I want to get closer to you, learn your secrets and report them back to Madison.* It seemed Bambi hadn't learnt her lesson, because like many times before, she was going to give the girl a chance.

"Okay."

Josh took long strides toward Courtney, Bambi now gone. She saw him out of the corner of her eye and gave him a smile. The glower on his face, caused her smile to fade away. Once he was in hearing range, she spoke "What's wrong-" He cut her off, speaking fiercely "What were you saying to Bambi?" A frown took over Courtney's face. The two of them hadn't spoken since their fiasco in his car and the first thing he wants to discuss is Bambi. She pushed away the burning feeling within her chest. Crossing her arms over her chest, she responded to his question "Nothing concerning you." Josh released a frustrated breath and ran a hand down his face "Look, Courtney. Just leave Bambi alone, whatever you're up to, stop it, it isn't going to change anything between us."

His words were like a slap in the face and she tried not to show they had affected her. "I'm not up to anything. I genuinely want to get to know her. Besides, why do you care so much? You barely know her." she spoke glaring at him. The frown on Josh's face grew deeper "The things I do is none of your concern. The point is, you do this all the time Courtney. Every time I show a little interest in another girl, you get crazy and possessive, driving the girl away. *We* are *not* in a relationship"

She adverted her eyes from his, as she felt them start to water. His words hurt her, she could admit that. Courtney knew she could get jealous and too overprotective sometimes, but she couldn't help it. Josh acted as if they *were* in a relationship. In private, he would comfort and compliment her. He was there for her and she was there for him. Isn't that how couples acted?

A horn honked. She heard Josh sigh "That's my ride. Look, things are getting out of hand between us. Maybe it's best if we take a break from one another. See you later, Courtney."

Courtney didn't look up or respond. Her mind was still trying to wrap around what she had just heard. He wanted to take a break? She knew by *break* he meant *breakup*. Courtney felt a pang in her chest. She wasn't ready to give Josh up, yet. He was all she had.

"Tsk, tsk. I hate seeing lovers fight. It just breaks my heart,"

Courtney looked up. A tear betraying her and falling from her eye. She furiously wiped it away. Madison's lips were formed into a sympathetic pout, but her eyes said something else. Courtney sniffled and glowered at the other girl "Not now, Madison. I'm **not** in the mood," she sneered, her voice faltering.

Madison's expression didn't change and she shook her head "I'm not here to taunt you. I've been through the same thing, so I know how it feels," she said, placing a hand to her chest. Courtney looked her over with squinted eyes "Really?" she asked, not believing her one bit.

Madison nodded her head and took a step to stand next to Courtney. She looked up at the sky, speaking "I remember how I felt, too. Betrayed, hurt, alone, angry, it was all too much." Courtney swallowed. That was exactly how she was feeling. Madison's signature smirk appeared "But, I used all those emotions to my advantage. I got back at the girl who was the cause of it. I mean it's only fair, right. If she hadn't been involved, then it wouldn't have happened,"

Courtney watched the girl, skeptically "What did you do?" A strange expression took over Madison's face, but only for a moment. In a blink of an eye, it was gone. Madison continued to look at the sky, as she spoke. "It doesn't matter. What matters is I got my revenge and it felt *good*," Courtney's brains began to whirl with thoughts. She shook her head to snap out of it. Madison noticed this, too and grinned "Don't fight it. It's okay to want revenge. Bambi deserves whatever you're thinking. If it wasn't for her Josh wouldn't have gotten angry and broken up with you, right?"

Courtney didn't respond, trying to ignore the girl "Aren't you mad? I would be, if I were you. Especially, if I cared for Josh as much as you do. You guys are perfect for each other. You going to let some girl who he barely knows take him from you?"

A car pulled up. Courtney was relieved it was for her. She looked at Madison and scowled "Whatever, Madison. I know what you're trying to do and you can forget it. You're not going to fool me."

Madison tilted her head and furrowed her eyebrows in confusion "Who said I was trying to fool you? If anything, I was trying to help you. Us girls got to stick together, right?"

Courtney rolled her eyes and turned around. Madison's words were still on her mind, as she walked to the car.

Your friends can be your worst enemies,

And your enemies can become your best friends,

All it takes is you to choose wisely,

A person will reveal their true colors within time,

It's up to you to decide if you wish to see or

continue on blindly.

CHAPTER SEVEN

Frenemies

Bambi walked into P.E. late, as usual. She noticed everyone was dressed and made her way to the locker room. It was empty. This was the reason Bambi liked to come to P.E. late. She didn't like getting dressed in front of the other girls and didn't care about the points that it caused her. She opened her locker and pulled out her clothes. A noise made her pause. Vomiting, followed by coughing could be heard from one of the stalls. Placing her clothes on the bench, she walked towards the noise.

She came to the stall and listened, as the person vomited, once again. This time the vomiting was followed by crying. Bambi chest rose and fell with a deep breath.

Instantly, feeling sympathy for the girl. The crying quieted to sniffles and the toilet flushed. Bambi raised her fist up to knock, but the stall's door opened, before she could get a chance to. Both girls stared at each other in shock.

Bambi's eyes wandered over the girl "Madison?" The other girl glared and shoved pass her. She sat her purse on the edge of one of the sinks. Turning on the faucet, she cupped some of the water and used it to rinse out her mouth. She then used the water to splash her face. Madison took a pack of mints from her purse and dumped a couple in her mouth. Feeling refreshed, she turned around. Her smile fell at the sight of Bambi.

She leaned back against the sink and crossed her arms. "You're still here?" she asked, after looking the girl over. Bambi said nothing, continuing to stare at her, silently. The look made Madison uneasy and she frowned "What are you staring at?" Again, the girl said nothing.

"Can't speak?" Madison was becoming irritated and uncomfortable "What's wrong with-"

Bambi finally spoke "A-Are you okay?" Madison eyes widened. Her face softened. She looked into Bambi's eyes seeing nothing, but genuine concern. Madison's face then hardened. *It's all a lie.* "You better not tell anyone what you just saw, got it" Bambi opened her mouth to speak, but then closed it. Her head fell and she nodded "Got it"

Madison walked out of the locker room and toward her friends. The smile on her face masking the true emotions she was feeling inside. Did Bambi think she could really trick her? Didn't matter. Madison wasn't going to fall for it. Bambi was a liar and not as innocent as people thought. *The incident* always reminded her of that when she would find herself falling for the other girl's schemes.

"What took you so long?" Tiffany asked once she was in range. Madison shrugged and flipped her hair over her shoulders "A girl's got to look good wherever she goes, right?" Tiffany shook her head, but still laughed. Behind her, someone spoke. "Hey, Madison," Madison turned around. She didn't recognize the boy, but smiled nonetheless "Hey,"

He reached behind him to rub the back of his neck "I was wondering if you were free this weekend," Madison tilted her head and assessed the boy. He was admittedly attractive, but she didn't know him nor did she want to go out with him. Still, it was good to have a list of many to choose from. *He could stay.* Madison bit her lip and frowned "Crap. I wish you would have asked me earlier, I have plans this weekend." It wasn't entirely a lie. She did have plans thanks to Ms. Clover and the school's stupid policy.

The boy's face fell in disappointment. Madison pretended to think and placed a finger to her lips "But. I might be free next Friday, is that okay?" she asked with a smile. The boy grinned and nodded "Fine with me." Madison giggled and pulled out her phone "We should exchange numbers, to keep in touch." The boy quickly nodded and the two of them proceeded to exchange numbers. Madison tried not to roll her eyes as they did so. The boy was too eager. "See you later, Madison." She waved and twisted back around. Madison knew she wasn't going to take things further than her using him, but he didn't. *It's alright, I always let them down easy.*

Madison was taken back by the look Tiffany was giving her. She placed a hand on her hip, cocking it out. "Have something you would like to say to me, Tiffany?" The rest of their friends turned to look at the girl. Tiffany rolled her eyes and uncrossed her arms. "How could you flirt with Tatum, Madison?" she asked. Madison's eyebrows knitted together "Who?"

Tiffany huffed "The boy you were just taking to." Realization hit Madison and she grinned. She walked over to stand next to Tiffany, throwing her arm around the pouting girl. "Aww, come on. Don't get upset, Tiff. I don't like the boy, I'm just using him. I'll give him to you as soon as I'm done, alright?" Tiffany scowled and knocked Madison's arm from around her. She stood up and went to sit away from them, pulling out her phone.

Madison remained calm, not letting the embarrassment and anger she was feeling, show. Their friends looked at them, worriedly. Madison forced a smile onto her face and waved them off. "Don't worry about it. Friends fight all the time, she'll forgive me in a couple of minutes. I think it's that time of the month" Her friends laughed and she joined in. Her laugh was just about as fake as their friendships.

Bambi walked out of the locker room and grimaced as all eyes fell on her. The incident between her and Madison had thrown her off, making her extra late. The rest of the students were gathered around the coach-who had already began to give out instructions. Coach Meyers frowned at Bambi "So, nice of you to finally join us. I'm not going to repeat myself, so try to listen to the rest and follow along." Bambi nodded and joined the circle.

Coach Meyers began speaking, again. A couple of girls moved to stand behind her. They spoke in whispers. Not loud enough for Coach Meyers to hear, but it was good enough for everyone else.

"I wonder what she was doing in there." Stephanie said, feigning curiousness.

Their leader giggled and spoke "I don't know, but who knows? With how long she took, it could've been *anything*. If you get my drift."

Students laughed quietly and Bambi continued to try to ignore them. It was hard and she began to feel herself start to shake a little bit. The girls didn't stop talking and continued to taunt her. By now, students had stopped laughing and were now growing uncomfortable. They could see the taunts were really starting to effect the girl.

Bambi walked along with everyone else onto the track. She hated the days they had to come to the track, but was grateful Coach Meyers gave them the option between running, jogging and walking. Bambi always chose to walk which lead to her being the last one to finish most of the time. Bambi walked the track, students running and jogging, passing her by. She didn't care. She used this moment to take in the scenery around her. RoseOak was really a beautiful place, if you chose to look pass its vindictive citizens.

Sun rays peaked through the trees, warming Bambi's skin. Sometimes, she would count how many birds she could find in the trees, to pass time.

"Hey. Bambi, wait up!" she turned around, as she heard her name being called. Courtney and Amber fell into step with her. Courtney gave her a friendly smile, before speaking "You walk pretty fast, you know? We had to jog to catch up to you" Bambi turned around and saw that she was indeed a good distance away from the track's starting point. The two girls walked alongside Bambi and she pretended it was normal, even though it wasn't. They talked amongst one another, as if the three of them had been friends for years.

Bambi didn't say anything and settled for just listening. Courtney released a frustrated breath and then spoke to her "What do you think, Bambi?"

"About, Ms. Monroe?"

The other girl nodded. Ms. Monroe was one of the strictest teachers in school. Bambi didn't mind that, though. As life went on, Bambi had learned that the strictest teachers were always the ones that had your best interest at heart. She didn't have any bad experiences with Ms. Monroe, so she didn't hate her as some of the other students did.

She settled for a shrug "She's never done anything to me." Amber gave Courtney a triumphant smirk. She rolled her eyes in return. "That's because you and Amber are a pair of goody two shoes, you both do *whatever you're told.*" She mocked. Had Courtney been someone else, Bambi would have thought the girl was trying to insult her. But, she could hear the playfulness in the girl's voice. *She's only joking, I think?*

Amber crossed her arms "It's better than being a convict." Courtney mouth opened in shock and she reached out to hit Amber's arm "Shut up. That was only one time, you were there."

"And, whose fault is that?"

"Please, you knew what you were getting into."

Bambi listened to the best friends bicker with amusement. They were like sister. It was clear that their friendship was strong. At one point of time, Bambi had known what it felt like to have a friendship like that. These days she hardly believed they existed. And she had one person to thank for that.

Suddenly, her body jerked forward, as someone shoulder-bumped her. Madison came to an abrupt stop, her groupies following. She placed a hand on her hip and smirked "Sorry. Didn't see you there." Bambi wondered if this was punishment for what she had seen in the bathroom. *A warning*. If Bambi spoke of anything she had seen earlier, Madison would make her pay.

Madison took threatening steps toward her "What can't talk" Before she could get any closer, a body stepped in between them. Courtney glared at Madison "Leave her alone, Madison. She isn't bothering you" The cheerleader's eyes widened innocently "I'm not going to do anything to her. I was just trying to apologize for accidentally bumping her." Courtney scoffed "As if, we all know you bumped into her on purpose." Amber just stood there, silently. Her face was expressionless, but also very intimidating.

Madison glared over Courtney's shoulder at Bambi "Need people to protect you now, Bambi. I thought we were all big girls, here." Amber crossed her arms "As did I, so what's the excuse for your childish behavior." Her expression then grew deadlier "Five against one, seems highly unfair, don't you think?" Amber wasn't a fighter and had no plans of changing that, today. But, she knew Madison and her friends were nothing, but dogs with more bark than bite. As soon as you lunged at them, they would go running. The other girl had started to shift under her stare and she knew she had won.

Madison felt herself becoming uncomfortable under Amber's gaze. She adverted her eyes "Whatever," she then turned to her clique "Let's go. This is stupid." She jogged away, but not without giving Bambi one last glare.

Amber and Courtney high-fived. Courtney eyed Amber "I think I have a crush on you, now." she said with a wink. Amber laughed and pushed her away. Bambi still stood behind them, silently. She wished they hadn't stood up for her. It would only bring them trouble.

Courtney noticed her silence and stared at her with concern "What's wrong?"

Bambi shook her head and began to fidget with her fingers "You shouldn't have stood up for me. Now, she'll start targeting you guys."

Amber scoffed "I'd like to see her try." she snarled and watched Madison and her friends.

Courtney nodded "Madison's a bully not an idiot. She knows me and Amber aren't afraid of her. She's not going to try anything."

Bambi sighed "You say that, now, but things can change. In fact, you shouldn't even be hanging around me. Why make your lives complicated?"

Amber released a breath "We've already told you we're not afraid of Madison. She can try to taunts us all she wants, it's not going to do anything."

Courtney scowled and placed her arm around Bambi "Excuse Amber's harsh way of explaining things. What she meant was you're our friend, now and friends are there for one another. Plus, once Madison sees that you've got people to back you up, she'll leave you alone."

Bambi wished it was that simple, but she knew Madison. It didn't matter if she had a hundred friends. Madison was never going to let the incident go.

"That's what I said!"

"I think you need to work on how you explain things, Am."

Amber turned away from Courtney offended, but then cursed. She pointed and they followed the direction of her hand. Half of the class had finished their laps. It was only them and a few students left. Courtney groaned "I really didn't want to run, today!" She took off, Amber and Bambi followed her laughing. Bambi was happy with this new found friendship. She only hoped it wouldn't be stolen from her within a night.

The gym was booming with noise, as the students waited for the bell signaling the period was over. Madison and her friends sat on the benches away from everyone. The girl was still seething over what had happened earlier. Courtney and Amber had no right jumping in to defend Bambi. *Why does everyone care about her so much, anyway?*

Madison's jaw clenched, as she watched Bambi laugh at something Courtney had said. She would let the girl have her fun for a while and let her think she had friends. But, it wasn't going to last long. She'd make sure of that.

"..Madison!"

She paused in her mental rant and turned to face Tiffany "Huh?" Her friend stared at her for a moment, bewildered. "You, okay?" Madison forced a smile on her face and flipped her hair over her shoulder "Of course, why wouldn't I be?" Tiffany and the rest of their friends shared a look. "You were out of it for a while there."

Stephanie nodded "Yeah, you haven't stopped glaring at Bambi since what happened at the tracks." The girl blew a bubble with her gum and then let it pop "What's up with you two, anyway?" You've been at her since freshmen year." Everyone waited for a reply, they were all curious themselves.

Madison held back her glower at Stephanie's question. The girl was just too nosey for her own good. *She'll have to go.* Madison glanced over at Bambi, then her friends "It's personal, leave it at that." Stephanie didn't seem to like her reply and crossed her arms. "You can't just expect us to accept everything you say with no explanation. We're not your puppets."

This time Madison allowed herself to glare, shooting daggers at the girl. "And, why do *you* care so much, Stephanie. You feeling sympathy for her, now?" she questioned, menacingly. The other girl swallowed, before she spoke. "N-No-Well, yes. I do, all of us do."

Madison tilted her head in thought. She looked around at each one of her friends. "Is that true? You all feel the same way?" They all avoided her gaze, none of them speaking up. *Poor, Stephanie.* Stephanie looked at her friends in disbelief that none of them would come to her defense. Madison clicked her tongue and turned to the shocked girl. "Looks like you're alone, Stephanie."

Stephanie snapped out of her shocked state and scowled at Madison "Come on, Madison. Even you have to admit we're a little *too* ruthless when it comes to Bambi. And, why? None of us know, but *you* do, and we deserve the truth."

Madison stood up and walked toward the girl, causing her to take a couple steps back "Fine. You want the truth?! There was a time when I didn't hate Bambi, but that was before she showed her true colors. To all of you she may seem innocent and pure, but that girl is vindictive and cruel. She'll do whatever it takes to make sure she's not hurt, even if it means someone else gets hurt in the process." Madison spoke every word with a snarl and clenched teeth. The girls listened, silently. Not sure how to respond or what to do.

The sneer was gone from Madison's face in a flash. She straightened herself out and smiled at Stephanie. The girl tried not to flinch. Tiffany knew that look and that nothing good could come of it. "But, don't worry, I'm not mad at you. You didn't know. None of you did," she said, glancing at the rest of them. Her eyes met Tiffany's and she winked, Tiffany sighed in return. *Poor, Stephanie.* Madison's eyes fell back on Stephanie and her smile grew bigger "Let's put this all behind us." Stephanie released a relieved breath and nodded.

The bell rang. Madison turned to walk away and they began following her. Abruptly, she stopped in turned to face Stephanie. The creepy smile still on her face.

"And by the way, Stephanie," The girl stopped, waiting for Madison to finish. The smile fell from Madison's face, turning into a sneer "You're out. Don't bother sitting with us anymore, today or the rest of the school year for all I care. Go make friends with Bambi since you seem to care about her so much."

Stephanie's mouth opened, tears whelming in her eyes "B-But...I..." she looked to her friends for help, but none of them would meet her eyes. They all felt sorry for her. But, their fear of Madison overlapped their sympathy for

Stephanie. None of them wanted to be in her place. None of them wanted to be the next target for Madison's wrath.

With that being said, Madison turned around walking towards the gym's exit. A smile appeared on her face as if nothing had just happened. Part of her felt bad for being so cruel to the girl that was once her friend, but she knew she had to. When you're this popular you couldn't show weakness. That gave people the advantage they needed to take you down.

Stephanie would thank Madison for this later. The girls hadn't stayed quiet out of their loyalty to Madison and she knew that. They feared her and she expected nothing less. Make people love you and they'll stab you in the back. Make them fear you and they'll never pick up the knife. The quicker Stephanie learned that, the better off she would be.

People hide their pain in different ways,

Through a smile or a laugh,

They pretend to be happy for those around them,

They'll hide their pain even if it's killing them,

Even if they're dying inside,

To them they're happiness doesn't matter,

But if you look a little closer,

You'll see that smile is forced and that laugh is

fake,

And that shine in their eye is actually a tear.

CHAPTER EIGHT

Pain

Bambi spotted her mother's car and practically skipped to it. For once, there was a smile on her face after leaving school. Today had been a surprise, but the good kind. She didn't have to eat or walk to her classes alone, and she found herself really enjoying the company of her new found friends. Amber had been right. Madison didn't have the courage to taunt her or Courtney, and now that Bambi was there friend, she didn't have the courage to taunt her either.

"What's got you so happy, today?"

Bambi tried to fight the smile that appeared on her face. Feeling anxious and excited, she told her mother about today's events.

Bethany listened to her daughter with a smile on her face. She was grateful today had been a good day for her. Most days, Bambi wouldn't even speak to her. She would just sit there like a statue. Quiet and expressionless. When she *would* talk, her words would come out as shouts. *Leave me alone*, is what she would say. To every question. It was always the same.

Bambi was a girl that liked to handle things on her own. Many would think it was nice having such an independent daughter, but it was both a blessing and a curse. At the end of the day, Bambi was just a girl. And, it honestly scared Bethany that she dealt with so many problems on her own.

"You should invite your new friends over, sometime. You guys can have a sleepover or go to the movies." Bambi's smile became a scowl. "Mom," she whined. "*Please*, I just met them, today. I can't just invite them over. They'll think I'm weird or crazy."

Bethany shook her head "That's what's wrong with you kids, now. You worry too much about what others think"

Bambi rolled her eyes, but the smile did not leave her face. Bethany took her eyes off the road for a moment and glanced over at her daughter. It had been a while since she had seen her daughter really smile. She just hoped it would last.

"I'm telling you son, I can see it. You're going to be a star. The best they've seen, all you've got to do is stay focused." Ace's father said, throwing the football.

Ace caught the football with ease and threw it back to his father. He pretended to be interested in what his father was saying, but the conversation mostly consisted of his father's dreams, not his. His father wanted him to be the school's quarterback. His father wanted him to continue playing football through college. His father wanted him to go to the NFL. His father wanted him to be the best. All he wanted was to be happy.

As days with on, Ace had begun to lose interest in football more and more. The sport had become less fun and more of a burden. He wasn't allowed to make mistakes like the others nor was he allowed to take breaks. Sometimes, he felt his father and teammates had forgotten he was human just like the rest of them.

"I got an A on my chemistry test." Ace said, trying to change the subject. His father caught the football, but did not throw it back this time. He held the football in his hands, his eyes narrowing for a moment. He shook his head and sighed.

"Try not to spend too much time on that stuff, son. You only need a C to play. Plus, recruiters don't focus on that stuff. They look at how good you are on the field not the classroom. Now, *that's* what you need to be focusing on."

The football felt heavier than usual, as Ace caught it. He realized it was just his exhaustion. After, many attempts it was clear his father wasn't interested in anything other than football. Still, Ace continued to try, hoping to find a *father* somewhere in there, not a coach.

"Hey, let's stop for, today. I forgot I have some homework to do."

His father caught the football and frowned "I thought you said you got an A? Come on, a few more minutes. You got good grades, a little homework isn't going to hurt you."

Ace shook his head "No, this is for math. I'm not doing too well in that. If I don't do the homework I might go from a C to a D."

His father closed his eyes and released a breath, his shoulders rising and falling. "Fine, but we're putting in extra practice, tomorrow." Ace nodded and grabbed a towel off a nearby lawn chair.

The kitchen was filled with the aroma of his mother's cooking. She could tell he was exhausted and handed him a glass of water. *He works the boy too hard.* Ace downed the water in two gulps. His mother rubbed his back and spoke, softly "You alright, sweetheart?" He shrugged and placed the glass of water down "Does it matter?" His mother sighed "You know your father, Ace." Her face was placed in a sympathetic frown. Ace nodded "Yeah, I know him. Football always comes first."

"That's not true." Ace raised in eyebrow in disbelief "Really? All he ever talks or cares about is football. How did you even end up with him?" Hurt flashed in his mother's eyes and he wished he could've taken the words back. It was too late, now. His mother smiled despite the sadness in her eyes "So, how are things at school?" she asked, changing the subject.

Ace didn't comment on it and shrugged "School's okay. Amber still won't talk to me, though." His mother rubbed his back encouragingly "Don't worry yourself, sweetheart. Things will work themselves out between the two of you. You guys had rushed into things, maybe she just needed a little break." He chose to believe in his mother's words.

Amber had been the only one who understood what he was going through. They both related to doing the things others wanted for them, rather than what they wanted for themselves.

"I'm going to go do some homework." He turned around about to head upstairs, but his mother stopped him. She handed him a small plate of cookies and placed a finger to her lips. Ace laughed and hugged his mother. He snuck up the stairs with the cookies, trying not to be caught. His father was strict about him eating sweets or "junk" as he liked to call it. The most he allowed Ace was the *organic* fruit snack gummies or chips. He would have a heart attack if he saw Ace so much as take a bite of a cookie.

"Hello, this is Amber Hart. I'm not able to accept your call at the moment, so-"

Ace tossed the phone on the bed. He sat on the edge of his bed, letting his head fall to his hands. At this point, Ace didn't know what more he could do. He had tried everything with Amber and it was clear she wanted nothing more to do with him.

He had lost Amber and now he was losing interest in football. Life was dragging him along and he didn't put up a fight. Graduation was coming up soon, and then what? He would continue to be Ace. Wanted by recruits who only cared about how good he played. Girls who saw him for how he could benefit them. Friends that solely fed off his status and popularity. A father whose dreams were the only thing that seemed to matter. There was one question that would never leave Ace's mind throughout all this. *Was it worth it?*

"Stop it, you little brat!" Courtney sneered, snatching the remote from her little brother. His lips trembled and soon he was crying, this caused her other siblings to cry also. Courtney groaned, throwing her head back. *Not again.*

"Courtney! Give the remote back to your brother!" Her mother shouted from the kitchen. Courtney frowned "But, I had it first!"

"I don't care! They're your younger siblings, so just give it to them!" Courtney rolled her eyes and shoved the remote back into her brother's hands. She stood up from the couch, heading towards the stairs, grumbling.

A pillow hit Courtney's face as soon as she opened the door. "Get out!" Her older sister-Caroline shouted at her. She was on the phone, most likely with her criminal boyfriend. Courtney crossed her arms and scowled "This is my room, too, you know?!" Caroline tilted her head "And? I'm the oldest, so you've got to do what I say. Now, get out!"

Courtney huffed and stomped her foot "Ugh! Things were so much better when you weren't here. Why can't you go back to Kyle's house?!" Her sister chuckled at her humorlessly "Are you done? Why are you bothering me anyway, don't you have to chase Jeremy or something?"

Courtney scoffed "Whatever. At least Josh isn't some delinquent. Didn't you catch Kyle with Ava?! And yet, you're still fooling around with him!"

Caroline's smirk fell. It was obvious Courtney's words had struck a nerve. She glared and stood up from the bed. Quickly, she walked over to Courtney, shoving her "Shut up! You don't know anything about us or our relationship. Yeah, Josh might not be poor or a delinquent, but that doesn't make you any different from me. You think you're the only girl he's seeing? Please, you can't even take care of yourself. Plus, Josh doesn't even acknowledge you as his girlfriend. You're not important to him. Just a quick fix."

Her sister stopped her ranting and looked her over. She placed a hand on her hip and smirk, reminding Courtney of another ruthless girl she knew. "You know, people say when you date someone it rubs off on you. I guess that's not the case for you." Caroline then slammed the door, leaving Courtney alone in the hallway. Tears fell from her eyes and she quickly wiped them away. "I hate you!" Courtney shouted, kicking the locked door. Her thoughts then drifted to Josh. She missed him, but no matter how much she would text him, he would not text back. She wondered what he was doing. It had to be better than being in a house full of people.

Like many nights before, Josh sat in the empty house alone. Isabella-their maid, had done her job for the day and went home. When Josh was little she would stay a little longer, but now he was older and she had a family. The emptiness of the house often suffocated Josh. It ate him alive, swallowing every little piece of hope. Feasting upon any happiness he had left, leaving behind broken promises and dreams. It craved for him to suffer a life without any warm hands to embrace him, or any shoulders to go cry upon. The only thing it wanted him to feel is the cold fingertips tracing his soul, getting close to him, yet still abandoning him in the end. The emptiness was the thing he feared the most, because he had no control of it.

His parents had divorced when he was younger. At the time he didn't realize what was going on. He supposed it was just another one of his parents' stupid fights. They would be back together in a couple days. Those days then turned to weeks, and weeks turned into months. When months turned into years, Josh had given up on his parents getting back together. He would just learn to deal with it.

He didn't realize he would be "dealing with it" alone. At the beginning, his mother would come and visit him during the weekends or let him spend the night over the weekend. Josh looked forward to those weekends. His father was never the compassionate type of parent and barely spoke to him. His life revolved around the company. As time went by, the visits stopped and Josh's mother no longer asked for him over the weekend. A couple months later, he discovered she was being married. Josh wasn't invited, but he had seen the pictures. His father had been the one to show him.

His mother had begun a new life, forgetting her old one. The one consisting of Josh. She didn't want her past interfering with her future, so she put it all behind her. Her child included. It didn't matter, because she had other children. She wasn't missing the one she had lost in the midst of a broken marriage.

When he sought out comfort in his father he was pushed away. If the conversation didn't include women or money, his father wasn't interested. He called it "Tough Love", but Josh thought of it as his father not knowing how to love. That was one of the many reasons his mother had left.

Josh had learned at a young age that you couldn't place your faith into people. He would have given up on people entirely, but someone's words still stuck with him. At times like this, he would remember those words.

*"Sometimes we're alone when we stand just to make sure we **can** still stand. Don't crave company when you're lonely, because most of the time it's not the good kind. Find out who you are and what makes you happy first. Then, when the right person comes along, you'll forget all about those days of loneliness."*

Josh vowed to never forget those words or the person who spoken them.

Amber's mother had put away the food and her brothers were preparing for bed, she too, was about to head off to bed when her father stopped her. "Amber. My office, now!" he demanded. She followed her parents to her father's office.

"Close the door" her father said, taking a seat behind his desk. Her mother took a seat on the small couch and she sat in one of her father's office chairs.

Breaking the intimidating silence, Amber spoke "Am I in trouble?" Her father shook his head "Not, yet." She waited for him to continue.

"Your mother and I have thought long and hard about this." Amber looked at them confused. *Thought about what?* "...We think it's time you move out." he said as if it was nothing. Amber's eyes widened. Her parents couldn't be serious "M-Move out...but I'm still in high school and-" her mother cut her off with a laugh. "Oh, sweetheart. You jump to conclusions too quickly. We're not saying you would be moving out, *now*. We're going to at least let you finish your last year of high school. And, it's not like you don't have anywhere to go. We've worked all of that out." she said. It didn't make her feel any better about the situation. Amber looked to the floor and shook her head "I don't understand…"

Her father pulled out a pamphlet and handed it over to her. Amber took it with a frown. Her frown deepened once she read its cover.

Amber looked from the pamphlet to her parents "So, when you said 'move out' you meant move *here*." she stated, glancing back at the booklet. Her mother pouted "Oh, try not to look so sad, sweetheart. This is an awesome opportunity and you should feel honored they're accepting you straight out of high school. Your father and I didn't get to attend until we were at least in our mid-twenties. This is an amazing opportunity, aren't you happy?"

Amber once again looked at the pamphlet and nodded, slightly "Yeah, it's wonderful." Her father's eyebrows knitted together, as he studied his daughter "Funny. You don't look pleased by it at all."

Amber shook her head "I am. Really. It's a great idea and a wonderful opportunity. But…This is a lot to take in and honestly…I don't think I'm ready." she said. It felt good to finally get it out. Her parents shared a look and her father sighed "Well, that's too bad. I've already talked to RoseOak and have set everything up. Do you know how that would look to be offered the chance of a lifetime by one of the top schools in the country and reject it?" her father chuckled humorlessly "It would be foolish and our entire family would be a mockery. It's time you grow up. So, if you are not ready, I suggest you get ready, because you *will* be attending RoseOak University next year, is that clear?"

Amber looked into her parent's eyes, pushing away the tears that had surfaced. "Yes. It's clear. I will be ready to attend RoseOak University by the end of this school year, I assure you" On that note her parents stood. Her father motioned for her to walk out and she did.

As soon as she was out of the room, Amber exhaled. But then, began to gasp and ran to her room in haste. Someone knocked on her door. "Who...Is it?" she gasped out. She couldn't stop the thoughts running through her head. "It's me. Are you okay?" her youngest brother asked from the other side of the door. *She thought of her parents demands.* "Yes...I'm fine...What do you need?" she asked through clench teeth. *She thought of all the pressure she was under.* "I had a nightmare. Could I sleep with you?" *There were so many eyes on her, so many voices speaking to her at once.* "No! Go away, Samuel! Go ask mom!" The little boy spoke, softly "I can't....They're fighting again" A sob escaped her mouth. *She wanted all the voices to stop and the eyes to leave.* "That's not my problem. Grow up and go to bed!" She felt like she would collapse any minute.

The little boy whimpered and a moment later spoke "Okay. I'm sorry. Goodnight, Amber…" Another sob escaped Amber's mouth, one she quickly muffled. Her heart was pounding against her chest, trying to escape. The room was no longer still. Amber sat on the floor, trying to calm herself. Trying to bring her brain and body back together. Nothing was working. There was only one thing left.

She ran to her bathroom and opened the medicine cabinet. Almost ripping the shelf off. She pushed pass everything to get what she needed.

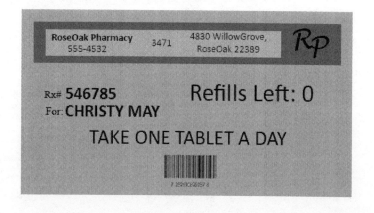

RoseOak Pharmacy
555-4532
3471
4830 WillowGrove,
RoseOak 22389
Rp

Rx# **546785**   Refills Left: 0
For: **CHRISTY MAY**

TAKE ONE TABLET A DAY

Amber paid the label no mind. She couldn't just have one. One was never enough. She opened the bottle and poured three in her hand. She downed them without water. Instantly, her body began to relax. Her heart no longer was trying to escape and remembered its place in her chest. She placed the bottle back in her cabinet-making sure it was hidden. She wasn't an addict she told herself over and over. She wasn't a drug abuser. She only used the pills when she needed to. *Which was often.* The pills were her only escape. No one had knew about them, but Ace. It didn't matter, though. They were no longer together, so she could no longer depend on him. She couldn't depend on anyone.

Sitting in her room, Bambi finished the rest of her homework. Today had been such a good day for her that she had even posted something on her CaptureMyLife account. Her phone buzzed, pulling her out of her thoughts. She unlocked her phone, but then instantly wished she hadn't.

COMMENTS

PrettyPrincess Awww....Little Bambi made friends....You wanna cookie? @GossipGuru @itshayday @TiffanyLawerence

itshayday Who want to b friends wit a slut. Not I said the cat! Lol. She lying! #boyfriendstealer #lamegirls #slut #slutneedstodie

GossipGuru Lol. You guys r crazy. Don't worry it won't last. Bambi doesn't know how to have friends. #slutwantsattention

TatumHowler Slut! Some girls just can't live without attention. It's really sad. Hit me up @GossipGuru

TiffanyLawerence You guys are so mean. Leave the girl alone. Good night, I'm logging off.

Add a comment...   Send

Bambi quickly deactivated her account, once again. She placed her hand up to her mouth to silent her cries. The harder she pressed, the more she hoped it would stop her crying. Bambi had different types of tears. Ones that showed sadness and ones that showed pain. But, the ones that weren't shed was the worst of them all.

There had to be something wrong with her. That had to be the reason. Why else would people hate her so much? She didn't understand. It's funny how people can give you a compliment and you'll forget it in a moment. They insult you and you'll remember it for a lifetime. But, bad often overlapped good or at least was more distracting.

This is where the bad part kicked in. Bambi could feel it. This unwanted feeling. It made her question her purpose, her existence. She was a prisoner in her own mind. With no will or knowledge of escaping. What was the point? She would just become locked up, again.

"Bambi! Dinner's ready, come eat!" Bambi wiped away her tears and looked in the mirror, hoping to fix her appearance. She tried smiling, but that only led to crying some more. Every time she looked in the mirror, it was the same, and she hated it. The mirror never lied, it always told her the truth. She was broken.

"Okay, Bambi. What's wrong? You've barely touched your food." Bambi shrugged at her mother's question and continued to look down at the table. "Nothing's wrong." Her mother sighed "Bambi you always say that. You're my daughter, I know something's wrong." She shook her head in response "I'm fine."

Growing frustrated, her mother threw her fork down "You are not fine! Something's wrong with you! Now, tell me what it is!" her mother demanded. Blinking away the tear, Bambi swallowed and explained everything to her mother.

Once Bambi was done explaining, her mother groaned "Bambi, I told you not to make a CaptureMyLife account. That social media's no good." Bambi tilted her head and stared at her mother for a moment. She chuckled, humorlessly and stood up from the table "Okay, goodnight."

Her mother stood up also, blocking her path "Goodnight?! No! We're talking, sit back down!" Bambi sighed and crossed her arms "I'm tired."

"Bambi, why?! Why must you do this?! Stop letting people tear you down, ignore them?! Don't let them destroy you!" Bambi wanted to laugh at her mother. Did her mother honestly think she *wanted* to be treated this way? To have people always attacking her. To spend nights crying herself to sleep or not sleeping at all. To be disappointed that she was waking up to see another day, because she knew what was to come. To crave death with a passion. People lectured that suicide shouldn't be an option, but for many it seemed like the only option.

Adults didn't know how much of a hell school could be. It was like walking into your ow demise, when you walked through those school doors. And, you were on your own every time, because in the end people pretended to care, but they really didn't. That's why people like Bambi pretended to be okay, even when they really weren't.

Bambi knew her mother didn't truly care about what she was going through. Her mother didn't do what she wanted her to do. It was the thing she hoped for every time she came to her with her problems. Comfort. She didn't want her mother to lecture her about what not to do. She had seen the effects of that.

All she wanted her mother to do was comfort her. To take her in her arms and assure her everything would be alright. But, she never did. So, Bambi never opened herself up fully. Because, if she did that, she was afraid that when she would once again be hit, it would break the last wall she had. Finally, drowning her in her own sorrow. So many people wanted her gone. Well, one day she might just give them what they wished for.

"Yeah, my mom's taking me on a trip to SilverBay Resort for my birthday." Madison lied, as she picked at her nails. Tiffany gasped and groaned *"Ugh! You're so lucky."* Madison giggled "I know, right?" Sometimes she would get so caught up in her lies that she believed them herself. "So, what type of swimsuit should I wear? I'm thinking about wearing a one-piece, my body sucks."

She heard Tiffany scoff *"As if, your body is literally goals. You should wear a bikini or something. The guys won't be able to keep their eyes off you."* Madison smiled in content. She loved her body, but she still got joy out of others complimenting her. *"Speaking of showing skin,"* Madison waited for her to continue.

"You know that new crop top I bought? The one you wanted me to give you. I think I'm going to where it to school Friday. What do you think?"

Madison rolled her eyes. *She's such an attention seeker.* "I mean you can, if you want to look like a slut that is."

"A slut?! How would I look-"

The sound of glass shattering cut Tiffany off, followed by shouts. Madison sat up in her bed.

"What was that-"

"I'll call you back, Tiff" Madison, spoke hurriedly. She jumped from her bed and ran out of her room. She walked down the hallway and the closer she got, the louder her mother's screams became. Madison peeked over the corner into the hallway, her eyes instantly watering at the sight.

Her mother laid on the ground as Frank-another one of her mother's "friends" continued to hit her. This would happen often. Her mother and her friends would get too drunk and then things would get out of control. Nights like this, Madison would just close her room door and lock it. But, this time she couldn't just ignore the screams. When Frank raised his foot to kick her mother, Madison hurried from her hiding spot and shoved him.

He didn't move much and it wasn't long before he struck her, also. Madison's mother saw this and jumped in between them, pushing Madison away. "Frank, stop! She doesn't know what she's doing! Don't take it out on her!"

Frank look from the both of them and clenched his jaw. "Whatever," he grabbed his beer off the coffee table, taking a sip "You're just a bunch of whores, anyway." He chuckled, walking toward the door.

When he left, Madison rushed to her mother. "Mom? Are you okay-" Her mother's hand met her cheek before she could speak. "Shut up! Just shut up! Look at what you've caused! Now, how am I supposed to pay the water bill?! Just go!"

Madison held her stinging cheek, staring at her mother with tears in her eyes "Mom….I'm sorry…I…" Her mother's glare sent shivers of fear through her "Didn't you hear me?! I said shut up, and go! Now, get out! I don't want to see you!"

Madison ran to her room and slammed the door. She walked toward her bed, picking up her phone and clicked one of the many numbers she had. Her mother wasn't the only one with "Friends".

"Hello?"

"Can you pick me up?"

"Sure, thing. But, only if you're up for a little fun."

"Have I ever called you for anything else?"

Madison was beginning to feel a bit of her sadness disappear. The movie ended and Mason used the remote to cut the T.V. off. He turned to Madison "So, you want to talk about why you called me to pick you up at 2 o'clock in the morning" Madison wasn't one for talking about her feelings and stood up.

"Not really, I could leave if you want me to, though." She teased. Mason's arm shot up to grab her "Okay, Okay. I didn't say all that. I was just trying to be a gentlemen."

Madison shook her head and gave him a peck on the lips "Well, don't. I don't like gentlemen. They're boring."

Mason chuckled "You shouldn't cry, you're too pretty for that." He said, caressing her cheek. Mason was one of the few guys that Madison actually enjoyed spending time with. Unlike the others, he was never in a rush to get her out of her clothes. She didn't think what they had was a

148

relationship. It was more like an agreement. He would give her attention and she would give him pleasure. They're lips met and Madison felt a weight lift off her shoulders, as she closed her eyes. "Want to watch another movie?" He asked against her lips. She shook her head. "No."

When his lips fell to her neck, Madison opened her eyes. She wasn't enjoying this and she wasn't going to. She never did. Its only purpose was to help her feel a little less empty, even if it was for a short while. Most girls wanted love and sought it out through men. Madison didn't want that. Love is what makes people weak. It's what makes people hate. Love is what makes women bitter. Love is what destroyed her mother.

Our thoughts and emotions,

The most dangerous things,

Because those thoughts and emotions lead to actions,

And actions often end with consequences,

Bad consequences lead to bad thoughts,

Bad thoughts lead to bad emotions,

Bad emotions can lead to bad results,

Blame our thoughts and emotions.

CHAPTER NINE

Dangerous

"I know, right?! I hate calculus."

Courtney rolled her eyes at Bambi's comment and tried to focus her attention on something else. In the past few days, Bambi and Amber had gotten closer than ever. Courtney would be lying if she said it didn't bother her. The more Amber and Bambi got closer, the less she felt she fit in. Conversations now consisted of school, tests, and studying. *And more studying and more studying.* Things Courtney just wasn't interested in.

The bell rang and they all stood up. Amber turned to her "We'll see you at lunch." Bambi smiled and said goodbye. The two of them then started walking to class together. Another irritating thing about the situation was that Amber and Bambi nearly shared every class together. They just hadn't been friends, so they never talked.

"Ugh! That's got to be so annoying."

Courtney twisted around coming face to face with Madison. The other girl walked toward her, followed by Tiffany. She stopped in front of her and gave her a sympathetic smile. "I don't know how you do it, honestly. I mean aren't best friends supposed to stay together?" Madison questioned.

Courtney frowned "Cut the crap, Madison. I know you're just trying to use me." Madison pouted "That's not it at all. I'm trying to help you. I don't know why, but I see myself in you."

"I'm nothing like you!"

Madison inspected her nails "Are you sure about that? All caused by one girl. Boyfriend breaks up with you.

Best friend betrays you. I've been through it all, before. And, I know how much it hurts."

Courtney tried to ignore Madison. She knew the girl just wanted to turn her against Bambi. But, Madison words were starting to get to her. In the course of a few days her life had taken a sharp turn. Things were no longer making since to her. *Could this all be Bambi's fault?* Courtney quickly cleared the thought from her mind. This is what Madison wanted. She hated Bambi and she wanted everyone else to hate her too.

Madison could tell her words were having an effect on Courtney and she smirked. She placed back on her fake expression of sympathy, continuing to speak. "You see, Courtney. We're more alike than you think. You'll come to us when you realize this and we'll be there for you. Just know, I'm not a girl that likes to wait too long."

"You wanted to talk to me, Coach?" Josh asked, as he entered the office. Coach Green motioned to the chair in front of him. Josh closed the door, before sitting down. He waited for the older man to speak.

Coach Green ran a hand down his face and released a breath. "I don't know what's going on with you and Woods, but whatever it is you guys have got to figure it out, because it's effecting the team."

Josh frowned in confusion. There was no problems between him and Ace. "What do you mean, Coach? What problems?" Coach Green sat back in his chair, his expression blank. "Come on, don't act like you don't know or haven't noticed it, Josh. Woods is one of my best players, yet he can't even throw a ball properly. And, you. For some reason you keep holding yourself back. I've seen you in practice. You score touchdowns like they're nothing, but during the games you barely score twenty yards. Ace is the quarterback and you're running back. You guys have two of the most important positions on the team, so they count on you. I've tried talking to Woods, but he's hardheaded and assures me it's nothing. So, are you going to tell me what's going on or lie to me, too?"

Josh was silent, letting his thoughts process. He had never thought of telling anyone about his problems. It was *his* problems, so he felt it was his job to deal with them alone. The thought of telling someone made him curious, though. Would that help him? Then again, telling someone could also have a bad effect on him. It could get his father in trouble. He would be completely abandoned, then. Still, it didn't hurt to take a chance. Josh took a deep breath, then proceeded to talk to Coach Green, hoping this wouldn't backfire on him.

Coach Green listened to everything Josh said with an unclear expression. "I grew up with your father, Josh. So, I don't find any of this hard to believe. I'm sure you want to make him proud, but you do not have to do that by putting your dreams on hold. A parent will love you regardless, that's their job. Even when they don't want to. I'm sure if you talk to your father he'll understand. And, if he doesn't, we'll be there for you. Though it might seem so, you're never alone, son. They'll always be somebody there to help you."

Josh walked down the hallway of the school, feeling lighter. He would be lying if he said the discussion with Coach Green didn't help him. He was now confident in talking to his father. Josh wanted to let him know what his real goals and dreams were. He didn't want to quit football nor take over the company. His heart wasn't in it. And, he would rather spend the rest of his life working hard for something he loved, rather than take it easy and be miserable for the rest of his life.

Josh was deep into his thoughts and accidentally bumped into someone. He shook his head clear and began to apologize. His apologetic smile turned into a grimace upon recognizing the person. A huge smile broke out onto Courtney's face "Josh! I-"

"Sorry, I can't talk right now." He said quickly, trying to maneuver around her. Courtney blocked his path in a haste. Her face was pulled into a scowl. "Why have you been avoiding me?" Josh felt a headache coming on and ran a hand down his face "Please, Courtney. I don't feel like arguing." The scowl left her face. Her eyebrows knitted together in a worried frown. She placed her hand on his cheek "What's wrong?"

Josh moved his face away from her hand "You." He once again, walked around her. He had made it a couple of feet away from her, before she spoke. "What did I do?!" she shouted, letting her emotions get the best of her. Josh was thankful the hallway was empty. He hoped Madison wasn't anywhere lurking around the corners.

Looking at Courtney, Josh could tell he let things go too far. It was clear in her eyes that what she felt for him was deeper than lust, but he didn't feel the same way. His relationship with Courtney was supposed to be the same as all the other girls. Strictly sexual. Courtney wasn't like the other girls, though. She didn't want extravagant gifts or money. All she wanted was someone to love her. Her only downfall was that she had looked for it in the wrong person.

He remembered her question and decided to finally tell her the truth. "You didn't do anything, Courtney. This is all my fault. I'm not perfect. I've got problems I need to conquer and I don't want them effecting those around me. Besides, I'm not good enough for someone like you."

A tear slipped from her eye and she hurriedly, wiped it away. "I don't care. I still love you." Josh's mouth tugged into a small smile. "I know. And, that's why you're too good for me."

Courtney could barely focus. Her thoughts were in a spiral. She wasn't understanding anything that was going on. Nothing made sense. Things were starting to change too fast and it was hard for her to keep up. Amber and Josh were two of the most important people in her life, and they were being torn away from her. All by the same person. Courtney was trying to be strong and not turn on Bambi like Madison wanted her to, but it was hard.

Amber was her best friend. They spent all their time and did everything, together. The time they spent together was now accompanied by Bambi. And, the things they usually did were forgotten. Not to mention Mr. Hart *liked* Bambi and he didn't like anyone.

When Courtney was upset, Josh would usually be the first person she confided in. Lately, she could barely get a reply to a text. Earlier, she could tell something was wrong with him and even attempted to console him. It was the first time he had rejected her comfort. Josh had never done that, before and Courtney knew there was only one explanation for it. Abruptly, she stopped. Glowering at the sight in front of her.

"Can you pass me a napkin?"

Ace nodded and handed Bambi one of the napkins. She thanked him and used it to wipe her face. Even though it had been a few days, now. Bambi still hadn't come to terms with her and Ace being friends.

They had grown closer since the day they had spoken about Peyton. Both of them were in need of someone they could confide in. A friend. From just one glance at the two of them, people might think that they were something more, but neither one of them saw the other in that way. Ace still possessed feelings for Amber that weren't just going to go away by meeting someone new and Bambi didn't have any interest in starting a relationship with anyone.

"Had any problems, today?" Ace asked, breaking the comfortable silence. He asked her the same question every day since their new found friendship. Reminding her of an older brother. Bambi shrugged "The usual." Ace sighed "You really should tell someone what's going on, Bambi." A sarcastic remark was her response. "I tell you." Ace gave her a look. There had been numerous times when he had volunteered to "take care" of her bullies.

Bambi didn't want him getting in trouble on her behalf, so she declined every time. She was used to the bullying. School would be over soon, so she knew she could deal with it until then. Ace shook his head "The more you wait, the worse it's going to get."

"It's okay, I'm used to it" she said, reciting her earlier thoughts.

"Just, because you're used to it doesn't mean you're okay."

"I never said I was. I said *it's* okay, meaning the situation. Now, enough about me. What's going on with you?"

"The usual. *Coach scolding me. Everyone depending on me to lead the team to victory. Dad's still focused on his dreams rather than my own.*"

Sometimes, Bambi had to wonder who had it worse. Her or Ace. People didn't really try to befriend her, so she was mostly alone, and that could be pretty *depressing*. Ace was wanted by almost everyone, though, so he was never alone, and that could be pretty *stressful*.

The two of them were different in many ways, but they were also quite similar. Misunderstood and alone. Bambi had been cautious to befriending Ace at first, just as he had been to her. They both thought their difference would cause a problem within the friendship, but it never did.

"I'm glad we're friends, Ace." He seemed taken back by her random comment, but nodded. He eyed her suspiciously, before speaking "Yeah….Me, too….But, don't go falling in love with me or anything. I mean you're attractive and everything, and I care about you, but I just don't see you in that way-"

"Really, Ace?!" A disgusted expression took over Bambi's face at his words. "First, I do not see you in that way. Secondly, I am definitely **not** going to fall in love with you. Thirdly, ew!" Ace scowled and turned away from her. "You didn't have to be so harsh about it." He mumbled. Bambi giggled and wrapped her arms around him. She apologized, leaning her head on his shoulder. Ace shook her off of him while laughing. "Okay, Okay. Enough. What did I just tell you?"

Bambi shoved him away, but still laughed. It felt good to have a friend.

Courtney knew Bambi was up to no good and what she had just witnessed proved it. No wonder Bambi was always being so nice to Amber. She wanted to get to Ace. Courtney wasn't going to let that happen. Bambi had her fooled for a moment, but not anymore.

She turned around and began speed walking down the hallway, ignoring the strange looks other students were giving her. She found Amber at her locker. Amber placed her books in her locker, giving Courtney a bewildered look. "You, okay?" Courtney waved her question away "I'm fine, but you might not be," Amber raised an eyebrow, waiting for her to continue. "It's, Bambi." Amber rolled her eyes, crossing her arms "Really, Court? Again? Have you been talking to Madison? How many times do I have to tell you? Bambi and I are friends, but you're my *best* friend. Nothing's going to change that."

"No, listen! Madison was right all along. Bambi's taking everything from me. You, Josh. It's not going to be long, before she does the same thing with you. She's already started with Ace."

"You're starting to sound like Madison, Courtney. Stop acting so paranoid about things. Besides, Ace and I aren't together anymore, so it doesn't matter. Now, come on, lunch's almost over."

Courtney frowned. She couldn't understand why Amber was trying to blow her off.

"You're supposed to be my best friend. Why don't you believe me?"

"It doesn't matter whether I believe you or not. I just choose not to get involve in drama. I have bigger things to worry about. Ever since Josh, you've changed into a different person and it's becoming exhausting, Court."

Courtney eye's turned to slits. She hated when Amber always went to the subject of Josh as if that was the root to all her problems. "You, know? I can see why Ace broke up with you, now. All you care about is yourself."

It was obvious Courtney's comment had struck a nerve by the reaction she got. Amber didn't know what was going on with Courtney, but she wasn't going to just submit to her, because she was being a brat. "And you don't care about yourself at all! All you ever care about is some guy, who doesn't even want you!"

Courtney's eyes widened in shock. Out of all the things, she had never expected Amber to say something like that to her. Not once in their friendship had she commented on the relationship she had with Josh. Courtney was beginning to question how strong their friendship really was.

She wasn't going to show Amber her words had hurt her. She frowned and spoke in a snarl. "Whatever, I don't need to get lectured by you! You think you're better than me, but you're not! It's my life and I'm going to live it the way I want to!"

Courtney didn't wait for Amber to reply and turned around, trying to get as far away from her as she could.

Alone and angry, Courtney sat at a lunch table by herself. She looked around the cafeteria, watching friends and couples interact. As she did this, she was starting to realize how lonely she really was. She wondered if this was how Bambi felt. She then shook her head free of the thought. Bambi might have felt like this in the past, but now she had gotten friends. Friends that didn't belong to her. Friends she had stolen.

Her eyes locked on Josh. She gave him a small smile, but he only shook his head and went back to talking with one of his teammates. Courtney glared down at the lunch table. *This was all Bambi's fault.*

A body sat down next to her, another one across from her. Courtney's mood only worsened upon seeing Madison's smug smile. With a sigh, Courtney addressed the meddlesome cheerleader.

"What do you want, Madison?"

She turned her head to look in Josh's direction, cocked her head to the side and gave Courtney a sympathetic pout. "First, she takes your bff. And now, your bf?"

"You must be pretty fed up by now" Tiffany said from next to her. Courtney tensed up, but didn't reply. Madison continued to speak. "I saw what happened between you and Amber in the hallway. And, it's obvious you and Josh are now having problems."

Tiffany smile and placed a hand on Courtney's shoulder. "But, we have a solution to that."

Courtney shook off Tiffany's hand. "No, thanks" She knew where this was going. Madison couldn't care less about her problems. The only reason she was interested was, because it involved Bambi. Madison's hate for the girl was still a mystery, but if it was similar to what Courtney was experiencing, she could now understand why Madison hated the girl so much.

"I think you should reconsider your answer. What's one thing your problems have in common?"

Courtney still didn't respond, even though she knew the answer.

"Bambi"

Courtney looked up and rolled her eyes. She sat back in crossed her arms. "Okay, let's stop with the games, Madison. I'm going to ask you one more time. *What do you want?* I know you're not here to just talk about my feelings."

Madison shrugged "Fine, you caught me. Truthfully speaking, your feelings mean nothing to me. But, there are a couple things I do want to talk about."

Courtney waited for her to continue.

"Pretend all you want, but I know what's going on is bothering you. You're losing two of the most important people in your life, because of some girl you barely know. Luckily for you, I'm on your side. Bambi may have other people fooled into thinking she's some type of angel, but I know the real her…." Her voice trailed off, as she got lost in thought.

The hate in Madison's eyes for Bambi frightened Courtney, even if it wasn't directed to her. Breaking out of her daze, Madison flashed Courtney a forced smile.

"So, what do you say? I can give you two options. Put Bambi in her place and get back what she's stolen from you or watch her walk away with something she was *never* supposed to have."

Courtney thought over Madison's offer. It was tempting and part of her felt what Madison was saying was right. If she did nothing Bambi would win. *She couldn't let that happen.*

Her eyes focused back on Madison and she looked the girl over. "What's the real reason you're doing all of this?"

Madison smirked. "That's not something you need to worry yourself about, we have a common enemy and two villains are always better than one."

Vengeance is in their heart,

So blindness is in their sight,

Nothing else matters to this person,

But the goal they seek,

At one point of time this person was hurt,

Vengeance is the only way to never again feel weak.

CHAPTER TEN

Vengeance

Bambi laughed as Amber complained about P.E. Today they would be running the track-a requirement. It also counted for half of their grade, so ditching was out of the question. She suddenly became silent and Bambi looked at her. Her eyes was focused on something and Bambi followed them, now understanding.

Leaning against the lockers, Courtney was laughing with a group of girls. But, that wasn't what had made them freeze. It was the person amongst the group of girls. "What is she doing with *her*?!" Amber sneered. Madison looked up and locked eyes with Bambi. Her wicked smile made Bambi look away. The cheerleader then started to walk in their direction, her groupies following her, with Courtney not that far behind.

Bambi grabbed Amber's wrist "We should go." Amber shook her head "No. That's what Madison wants. If we run away, she'll only continue to taunt us." Bambi sighed "And if we *stay*, things could get a lot worse."

Amber opened her mouth to reply, but stopped once Madison stood in front of them. Bambi's eyes shifted to Courtney and she could barely recognize her. The makeover she had been given made her look like a clone of Madison and a member of her entourage. Amber must have been thinking the same thing. The two of them shared a look.

"Well, if it isn't the backstabber." Amber ignored Madison's insult and looked at Courtney. Her eyebrows were raised and she looked from Courtney to Madison. "Really? We have one fight and you're ready to turn on me?!" The hurt and anger in Amber's voice made Courtney flinch.

She opened her mouth to respond, but Madison cut her off. Crossing her arms and stepping in front of Courtney. "Why are you taking your anger out on her? Your best friend. *She's* the problem," Madison sneered in Bambi's direction. Bambi's eyes fell to the floor and she turned to leave. Amber grabbed her arm, stopping her.

"No, she's not! You are, Madison! And everyone knows this, but they're all too afraid of you to say something, but I'm not. I know you're nothing, but a girl who likes to use her words to manipulate people. Deep down, you're just as scared as the very people you bully."

Madison's expression softened for a moment, but then her frown returned "You should watch that mouth of yours or-"

Amber laughed "Or what? I'll end up on that stupid blog of yours. Go ahead. The only people that care about the stupid things you put on there are just like you. Pathetic and ignorant."

Madison frowned and took a step toward her, but a body came in between them.

Ace was frowning down at her "Amber's right, Madison. You're starting to take things too far. Sooner or later someone's going to retaliate and it might not be with words."

Madison chuckled humorlessly. "You, two? Why am I not surprised? Little Bambi can't stand up for herself as usual." she looked around Ace to glare at the cowering girl. "You may have everyone else fooled, but don't forget I know the real you. And, it won't be long before everyone else does too" With that being said, Madison turned around and stomped away. Her entourage followed her, Courtney too, but someone grabbed her.

Josh didn't give her time to respond, before he marched off, tugging her along. Leaving the three of them alone. Amber watched them leave, before turning around. A scowl was on her face, as she looked up at Ace. "I didn't need your help. Next time, stay out of it." He rolled his eyes with a scoff "Yeah, Amber. You never need *anybody*. Besides, it wasn't you I was standing up for. I stopped trying a long time ago. You made it very clear that's what you wanted."

The harshness in his voice shocked her. Ace instantly regretted what he said, upon seeing the sadness in her eyes. Trying to hide her emotions, Amber's looked to the ground. Ace made a step toward her, but she didn't give him time to apologize. Turning on her heels, she took quick steps down the hall.

Ace watched her disappear around a corner and sighed. He hadn't meant what he said. Amber's words had hurt him and in the heat of the moment, he wanted to get back at her. He hated the flashbacks he would get of the two of them, and realize things weren't the same anymore. He'd give anything to get things back to the way they used to be. His mind always wondered if she thought of him as much as he thought of her or if he was insane for holding on to these feelings. Feelings he wasn't sure were requited.

"Are you okay?"

Bambi looked up at him worriedly. She knew how strong Ace's feelings were for Amber. Seeing the two of them push each other away was disheartening. Even though it wasn't her place, a part of Bambi wished she could help with the matter.

Ace ran a hand over his head and nodded "Yeah, you?"

She was anything, but fine. The incident with Madison and Courtney was obviously her fault. Courtney wouldn't have been with Madison in the first place, if she hadn't befriended her. Bambi also worried the argument between Amber and Ace would put a strain on their friendship. *Would she join up with Madison and Courtney?* Things would have been better if she would have just kept to herself.

"I know what you're thinking. It's not your fault."

Bambi shook her head "Everyone was fine, until I came along." Ace walked over and placed a hand on her shoulder "Everyone was *pretending* to be fine, you just made them aware of it."

"Ouch, Josh let me go! You're hurting me!" Courtney shouted, snatching her arm out of his grasp. She held her arms to her chest and massaged it, hoping to get rid of the pain. "What is wrong with you?!"

Josh grin and chuckled humorlessly "What's wrong with me?! I should be asking you the same question!" the grin was replaced by a frown. Courtney took a step back. She had never seen Josh this way, at least never with her.

"I-I don't understand."

Josh rolled his eyes and took a deep breath "Of course you don't. You never understand, Courtney. You always do things without even attempting to think them through. Because, of some stupid jealousy. You're hanging with Madison of all people and acting like someone you're not."

"Well, I wouldn't have to act this way if you would just treat me better! Not like sex is the only thing that matters between us!"

"Sex was always the only thing that mattered! I made that clear from the beginning. And, you didn't have any problems with it."

His words were like a knife in her heart, but she wasn't going to let them get to her. This wasn't her Josh. The Josh she knew wouldn't say these things to her. It was obvious he was going through something and she was going to get to the bottom of it.

She took a step toward him and tried to pull him into a hug. He grabbed her arms, placing them down and put distance between the two of them. Courtney scowled at his rejection of her comfort.

A stern expression was on his face, as he spoke "No more of that. No more running back and forward between each other. I have bigger things in my life I need to focus on and *this* is only going to hold me back. We're over and for good this time. It's for the best."

Her body instantly became numb. She didn't feel his hand pat her on the shoulder nor the tear that fell down her cheek. The water in her eyes made her vision blurry, and she could barely make out his departing figure.

The pain in her arm couldn't compare to the one she was feeling, now. Madison was wrong. She wasn't hurt. Now, she was angry. First, her best friend betrays her and now the love of her life wants nothing to do with her. And all this was thanks to one girl. Bambi had caused too much trouble in her life and she wasn't going to just sit back and let her. Madison's plan wasn't going to be enough to satisfy her vengeance. Bambi had to suffer. And, since so many people wanted to take her side, they could suffer right along with her.

Amber was aware of the discreet glances Bambi kept giving her. But, whenever she would look over at her, the other girl would look away. Placing her pencil down, Amber turned around to face Bambi fully. She was determined to get to the bottom of what was bothering the girl.

"Okay, cut the act. What's wrong?"

Bambi's eyebrows rose and she shook her head. "I don't know what you're talking about." She then went back to studying for an upcoming test. Amber rolled her eyes and pulled the book away from her.

She gave Bambi a stern look "I know something's wrong. Now, spill it." Bambi sighed "You're not mad at me, right?"

Amber frowned, not understanding why she would ask her that. She hadn't shown any signs she was mad at the girl. But, this wasn't new. It was obvious Bambi wasn't used to having friends. She would always ask questions to reassure that she wasn't doing anything wrong in friendship. Amber thought it was both sweet and sad.

"Why would I be mad at you?"

Bambi watched her fingers, as she fumbled with them. "Well, you and Ace got into an argument, because of me. He and I hangout a lot, but I don't want you thinking that I'm-"

"Bambi, relax. Ace and I always argue like that, it's nothing new. I'm not mad at you. Not everything bad that involves Madison is your fault. Madison and those who choose to follow her are bad all on their own. The havoc they cause in people lives are always intentional. In trust me. Even if you weren't here they would be doing the same things."

In the beginning, Amber never paid Madison any mind. It was ninth grade, so Amber thought Madison was just one of those girls that just did things for attention and popularity. The more time went by and the older they got, Amber started to understand why everyone hated Madison so much. The girl was a she-devil. And soon, she would see how bad the effects of her actions were.

"You know he's still in love with you." Amber woke up from her daydream and stared at Bambi with bewilderment.

"Who?"

Bambi threw her head back and groaned. "Who else is there? Ace!"

Amber felt her cheeks warm and looked away from Bambi. Her statement had made Amber feel awkward. She was sure Ace wasn't in love with her. Not with all that had happened between them. Besides, it wouldn't even matter if he did. It wouldn't work out. Their lives were too different.

"Ace and I aren't going to get back together. Our lives are too different. Being in a relationship will only distract me."

Bambi covered Amber's hand with hers. "I think you're too hard on yourself sometimes, Amber. Why?" She laughed in response and Bambi frowned. "I'm serious, Amber. It's okay to take a break sometimes. You're human."

The amusement disappeared from Amber's face and she opened her mouth, but was interrupted. Mr. Hart opened the door, poking his head inside. His eyes shifted from the closed books to them. He crossed his arms and raised an eyebrow.

"Mind explaining this? Aren't the two of you supposed to be studying?"

Bambi's eyebrows knitted, together. The severity in Mr. Hart's voice didn't remind her of the man she had just spoken to earlier. Amber hadn't attempted to respond, so she did.

"We were just taking a break, Mr. Hart. We've be studying all day-"

"And, that is how you get to the top," He said cutting her off. "Not frolicking or taking breaks. Breaks are for the weak."

"But-"

Mr. Hart raised a hand, silencing her. "Look, Bambi. I approved of your friendship with my daughter, because I thought it would be in asset to her. You seemed both intelligent and focused. But, one thing I will not tolerate is distractions. So, if that's what you're going to be, you can forget about this friendship."

Bambi's mouth fell open in shock. Mr. Hart waited for her to respond, but she didn't know how. Frozen in shock and fear.

Amber released a silent breath and looked up at her father. She forced a smile and laughed "Dad, We were only taking a small break. Bambi isn't used to my study habits. I know how you feel about slacking, so I promise not to let it happen again."

He looked over at Bambi and she quickly nodded. Seeming satisfied, he looked them over a last time and left.

Bambi couldn't believe what had just happened. She looked at Amber, but she wouldn't meet her eyes. In that moment, Bambi felt horrible for previous assumptions she had made. When Bambi had first started hanging out with Amber, she had envied the other girl's life. Wishing she could switch it with her own. It was true what they say. Never judge a book by its cover or a perfect girl in this case.

"*That* is why I'm so hard on myself. In this family, you can't show weakness or be *human*."

The vibrations of the loud music ran through Courtney, as she walked through the clustered house. Strobe lights flickered around. It helped illuminate things that were trying to be hidden by the darkness. In the past, Courtney would have never expected herself to be in a place like this. But, things were different now and so was she.

Madison followed Courtney and her friends to an empty couch. It reeked with the smells of cigarettes. She made sure no one was around, before she leaned in to whisper.

"So, I was thinking we change a few things?" Madison took a sip from her cup and raised an eyebrow "What do you mean? Change what things?" Courtney rolled her eyes. "With the plans. I think we're going too easy on Bambi. She needs to suffer."

Madison's eyebrows furrowed "Look, I understand that you're mad and everything, but it seems like you're taking things too far."

Courtney glared "Or maybe you're just too weak." Girls around them conversation died. Madison handed her drink to Tiffany and crossed her arms. "Excuse me?" A smirk made its way onto Courtney's face. "You heard me. You're weak. If you really hate Bambi as much as you say you do, you would be doing everything in your power to bring her down. Instead you settle for spreading petty rumors."

Madison stood up "Look-"

Courtney stood up also, cutting Madison off. "It seems you're more bark than bite, Madison. And, I can't have you holding me back. So, continue on with your little plan of revenge. Leave it up to the big girls to handle the tough stuff."

With that said, Courtney gave one last smirk and walked off.

Madison watched Courtney leave with dismay. The girl was quickly turning into something even worse than her. Tiffany turned to Madison and they shared a look. "We're going to have to watch her."

Courtney pushed her way through the crowd, following the sound of shouts and laughter. A girl was chugging down a bottle of alcohol, as people around cheered her on. Feeling eyes on her, she looked around, locking eyes with Tatum. Courtney grinned and made her way over to him.

"You know it's rude to stare." Tatum laughed and shook his head "With that dress on, how can I not?" Courtney looked Tatum over and tilted her head "I thought you were with Madison?" He took a step closer to her. "And I thought you were with Josh."

Courtney's grin grew wider. She looked around the party, before focusing back on him. Her eyes falling on the red cup in his hand. "What you drinking?"

He shrugged "Just some vodka?"

"Mind if I have a sip?" He shook his head and held the cup out to her. Like a moth to a flame she took it. Without thinking Courtney downed half of the contents inside the cup. Tatum took the cup away from her and placed a hand on her back. The taste was horrible, but the burn of the beverage had her reaching for more. "Be careful, it's pretty strong."

Courtney paid no attention to his warnings and finished the rest of the drink. It wasn't long, before she started to feel its effects. A giggle escaped her lips. Tatum was saying something, but she could barely understand what he was saying.

The music changed and more teens made their way onto the dance floor. Courtney watched them with satisfaction. This is where the good became bad and where the bad lost any bit of the good they had. This is where she belonged. Courtney grabbed Tatum's hands and placed a kiss on his cheek "Dance with me."

He nodded and led them to the dance floor. There was barely any room to dance, but they still found a way to. Suddenly, an idea popped into Courtney's mind. She leaned up to whisper into Tatum's ear, as they moved against one another. Her intentions were vile, but the yearning of revenge helped push her through it. "I need a favor. You play football, right?"

It didn't take much to get Tatum to agree. Her plan was slowly falling into motion. Everyone that betrayed her was going to pay. The old Courtney was weak and naïve. She was going to make sure never to be that girl again.

A long dark tunnel is what these people are,

With no light at the end,

Or remorse for the things they say and do,

They continue to wallow in their darkness,

With pity for themselves,

Everyone is to blaim for their problems,

Because a souless person has no idea on how to solve them.

CHAPTER ELEVEN

Soulless

Ace groaned and laid his forehead onto the table in defeat. Bambi frowned and placed her textbook down. Leaning forward, she repeatedly poked him with her pencil. "Come on, it's not that bad." Ace sat up and glared down at the work in front of him. "What's the point of this stuff, anyway? It's not like we're going to actually use it in life." Bambi laughed and sat back in her seat "The point is they don't care if we use this or not in life. But, if you want to get in a good college, you should put an effort into learning this stuff."

A faraway look appeared onto his face. "It wouldn't matter anyway." He looked in Bambi's direction and as if realizing what he had just said, straightened up. He released an awkward laugh "What I meant is…my grades are decent enough. As long as I'm not failing I can play football. And, as long as I'm playing football, I won't have to worry about paying for college."

Bambi sighed and picked up her textbook "But, is that what *you* want?" He shrugged in reply "It doesn't matter what I want."

"Yes, it does. Why would you want to spend the rest of your life doing something you hate?"

"What else am I good at?!"

Students around them looked up from their table at Ace's outburst. They watched them for a while, before returning to studying. Whispers could be heard and it was obviously about them. Ace lowered his head "It's not like I have options. Football is the only thing I'm good at. What other choice do I have?"

Bambi grabbed his chin, lifting his head up. "That's not true, Ace. Football isn't the only thing you're good at. It's just the only thing you've tried. I'm sure if you did other things, you'd find something you're good at. Just give it time."

Ace thought over her suggestion and nodded "I'll think it over. Seems kind of pointless when the school year's almost over." Swiftly, Bambi reached over and smacked his head.

"Ow! What's wrong with you?!"

Bambi sat back and crossed her arms smugly. "It looked like you were thinking about giving up, so I got rid of that thought!" she exclaimed, proudly. The librarian stood up and shushed them. Bambi ducked down and quickly picked her textbook up. She made sure the librarian wasn't watching them and spoke.

"Speaking of giving up...." Ace raised an eyebrow. "....IthinkyouandAmbershouldgetbacktogether." Her words were rushed, but Ace understood them perfectly. He flipped a page in his book and answered her conclusively "Not going to happen."

"Come on, you guys can deny it all you want, but I know-"

The stern look he gave her stopped her rant. Bambi slouched in her seat, glowering. Ace's scolding wasn't going to stop her from meddling. It still angered her that he wasn't going to try and hear her out, though.

"Hey, Bambi?" The scowl still remained on her face, as she met his eyes. "Yeah?" Ace tried not to laugh at her, but couldn't stop the grin that took over his face. "Thank you. For your advice, earlier. I needed it." Bambi's face softened and she gave him a soft smile "You're welcome. *Just don't go falling in love with me.*"

The warning bell rang, but Josh made no attempt to move from his spot on the school bench. Yesterday, he had planned on confronting his father, but got nervous and didn't go through with it. *What would the outcome be?* That was the question Josh always asked himself. It was hard to tell with a father like his. Normal teenagers would have faith that their parents would want them to follow their dreams, but he wasn't normal. Over the years, a wall had formed between him and his father. A wall that only allowed severity and separated real feelings or emotions.

"Are you okay?"

Josh's head shot up. His startled eyes met Bambi's worried ones. She broke eye contact and cleared her throat. "You don't look too good. Do you want me to get the principal or…."

Josh chuckled and shook his head. "I'm fine. Just have a lot on my mind. Thanks for the concern, though." She nodded and was about to walk away, but paused.

"Are you *sure* you're okay?"

Josh contemplated telling her 'yes' again, but then was reminded of a memory. In the past, Bambi had helped him through his dilemma. He didn't see the harm in talking to her. Unlike the other students, he couldn't see Bambi gossiping about his problems. Josh was still a little taken back, though. Bambi was the last person he expected to try and comfort him.

"Actually, there is something I'm having trouble with."

Bambi looked around and made sure no one was watching them. That would only make things worse for her. When she was satisfied that no one was paying them any attention, she made her way over to him.

She joined him on the bench "Is it school? I've been tutoring Ace, I could tutor you too if you want."

"It's not that. My grades are fine. It's my dad. There's something I want to tell him, but I don't know how." Bambi's eyebrows knitted together "You're his son, so I'm sure he cares for you. He'll understand."

Josh laughed humorlessly "You obviously don't know my father. He could give a care less about me. There's only one thing he cares about in this world." The more he talked, the harsher his tone became. Bambi could tell Josh held some resentment to his father and whatever relationship they had wasn't a strong one.

This once again opened her eyes. Bambi had judged both Amber and Josh. To her their lives were perfect. But, now that she was given a closer look inside, she was able to see just how dark it was.

Bambi touched his shoulder, making him look up at her. "I think you should still try. You never know, your father might surprise you. We have to face our fears or else they'll continue to chase us."

Josh listened to her, finding courage in her advice. He then grinned "Still haven't changed."

Bambi was taken back by his unusual reply and didn't know how to respond. Josh realized his thoughts had been said out loud. They sat in an awkward silence for a while, until Bambi interrupted it. "You know? You're nothing like I expected you to be. I shouldn't have judged you and I'm sorry for avoiding you all the time."

He waved her apology away "It's understandable. The burden popularity brings can be pretty tough sometimes." Bambi scoffed "You should try being an outsider." Her head suddenly snapped into his direction.

Bambi squinted her eyes and appeared to examine him for a moment. "You're friends with Ace, right?" Josh didn't know where this was going and responded nervously. "Yeah?"

A huge smile took over her face "Great, because I'm going to need your help with something! It's about him and Amber…"

Josh watched Bambi as she rambled about her plan to get Amber and Ace back together. It kind of made him jealous that Ace had a friend that cared so much about him. But, he also wondered what it would feel like to have that.

Madison stood outside the cafeteria doors, tapping her feet irritably. "Where are they?!" she exclaimed. Ten minutes had passed and there was still no sign of the other girls. There wasn't a single day when they didn't meet up. Tiffany checked her phone and sighed "I've tried calling them, but no one's answering." Madison was starting to get a bad feeling. Tiffany looked around and shook her head "Times running out. If we don't go in now, we'll miss lunch. Let's just forget about them. Maybe something's come up."

Madison's head snapped in her direction "Like, what? All of them just decided to miss school and get sick at the *same* time?!" she sneered. Tiffany just rolled her eyes in response deciding not to respond to Madison's dramatic behavior.

Familiar voices caught their attention. Tiffany's eyes widened at what she was seeing. She could only imagine how Madison was feeling at the moment. Her attention went to Madison and she was right. The other girl was fuming. Tiffany took in a deep breath and waited to see how things were going to transpire.

Courtney looked away from the girls surrounding her and looked in their direction. She smirked and started making her way toward them, beckoning the girls to follow.

She stopped in front of Madison and crossed her arms. "Well, what do we have here? Were you guys waiting for us all this time?" her voice was sympathetic and sinister at the same time. Madison didn't reply, so Courtney continued to speak. "The girls and I decided to eat off campus, today. We would have told you guys, but we know how stubborn you can be. None of us would want to end up on that *terrifying* blog of yours. Right, girls?" As on cue, they all laughed.

Madison stood frozen, not knowing how to respond. It was as if she was looking into the mirror. One that showed a crueler version of herself. Courtney took Madison's silence as a victory and strutted up to her, until their faces were inches apart. She then leaned down to whisper into her ear "There's a new queen bee in charge, Madison. The sooner you except that the better off you'll be."

Courtney backed away and turned toward the cafeteria doors. She was on her way into the cafeteria when she stopped and twisted her head. "Oh. And I would forget about *Gossip Guru* if I were you. People aren't really scared of it anymore. Fake rumors and childish gossip? It's just so middle school don't you think?"

Madison clenched her fist and grinded her teeth. Courtney-a girl who was just a nobody a few days ago, had rendered her speechless. Madison's breathing began to pick up and she knew what was happening. *I have to get out of here.* Tiffany attempted to follow her, but was stopped. Madison turned around with a scowl and shouted at her. "Ugh! Don't follow me! Why don't you get your own life and stop trying to be up under me all the time?!"

Madison didn't care about the problems her words would cause at the moment. Tiffany was one of her closet friends and would forgive her. She had bigger problems to worry about. Things were changing too fast and she was having a hard time keeping up. For as long as she knew, it had always been her job to throw people's lives off balance.

She always started the problems. Never had she experienced them.

Madison made it to the girl's restroom and rushed inside. A couple girl's stood by the sink and straightened up upon seeing her. The tears in her eyes shocked them. One of the girls spoke up "M-Madison? Are you alright?" More tears fell from her eyes and she roughly wiped them away. "Get out." The girls continued to stay frozen in place, watching her.

Madison released a deep breath and threw down her bag "I said get out!" The girls jumped and hastily rushed out of the restroom. Madison closed the door once the girls were gone. She walked up to the sinks and stared into the mirror. Her makeup was ruined from crying and her hair was a mess. The sight made her cringe. Looking into the mirror helped point out all of her imperfections. No matter how many times she tried to get rid of them, they always came back. Once she fixed something she didn't like about herself, a new flaw would arise. There was no winning.

She thought back to the comment someone had made on her page a couple days ago. They said she was starting to gain a little weight and suggested she go on a diet, but she didn't have the time for a diet. Diets took too long. She had a better method.

The warning bell had rang and Bambi was on her way to class, but something stopped her. She pressed her ear closer to the girl's restroom door and listened. Sobbing and sniffles could be heard. Someone was crying. She pushed the restroom door opened and made her way inside. The person was now vomiting and Bambi rushed to the stall it was coming from. Not prepared to see the person behind it "Madison?"

The other girl abruptly ceased her crying. She glared at Bambi and stood up from the ground. Madison used the back of her hand to wipe at her mouth. "You better not tell anyone about this" she sneered. Bambi shook her head "I won't, but are you okay? Do you want me to take you to the nurse or-" her speech was cut short by Madison's humorless laugh. "Yeah, right. As if you care. You don't have problems like the rest of us. You're *perfect*." her voice oozed with hate.

Bambi flinched at Madison's words. She opened her mouth to speak, but was cut off. Madison shoved her, as she exited the stall. She picked up her bag and gave Bambi one final glare, before leaving the restroom. Bambi stared off lost in thought. *I'm not perfect.*

Five minutes had passed and Bambi hadn't made any progress. Her nerves were getting the best of her. But, she knew this was something she had to do. The sight of Madison crying had did something to her. It took a lot to make the girl cry. This caused Bambi to realize things were deeper than just their dispute. Madison was going through something. Bambi hoped that if she helped get rid of that problem, Madison would give up causing trouble in other's lives.

Building up enough courage, Bambi took a deep breath and entered the office. The lady at the front desk looked up from her computer and smiled at her. "Hello. What can I do for you?" Bambi returned the woman's smile and shook her head. "Oh, nothing really. I just came to speak with Ms. Clover about something."

The woman frowned "Ms. Clover? I'm sorry, dear. She's not in today." Bambi sighed, but wasn't going to allow herself to give up. "Okay. I'll just come back tomorrow." The woman once again shook her head. "I'm afraid she won't be here tomorrow either." It was Bambi's turn to frown. She couldn't tell if the woman was being sincere or sinister. "Well, when will she be back?"

The woman shrugged "None of us know. She hasn't been to work since the death of her son." Bambi's eyes widened in disbelief. "Her son?" *Ms. Clover's son was dead?* She didn't even know Ms. Clover had a son. The woman nodded, sadly. "Yeah, He killed himself a while ago…" Bambi could no longer hear what the woman was saying. She could feel herself becoming nauseous and tried to push away the arising tears. Swallowing the emotion built up in her throat, she spoke. "W-What was his name?"

The woman stopped her speech and met Bambi's eyes. She gave her a sympathetic smile and answered. "His name was Peyton."

Bambi had decided to ride the bus home. She couldn't think straight upon today's revelation. Ms. Clover- the happiest person she had ever met, had lost her son. She had lost her son due to suicide. Bambi wondered if Ms. Clover had seen the signs. Depression was hard to fix and hard to notice. Bambi had saw that Peyton was depressed upon their first meeting. But, then again. Depression knows other depressions.

She wanted to check on Ms. Clover and make sure she was okay. Losing a child has got to be traumatizing. There was no way of checking on her, though. She wasn't coming to school and it was against school rules to give out personal information.

Bambi made her way to the front door and opened it. She opened her mouth to acknowledge her mother of her presence, but shut it. Her mother could be heard talking in the kitchen. Hearing no other voice, Bambi assumed she was on the phone.

As Bambi got closer, she could hear her mother's conversation more clearly. Her mother cried while trying to speak properly to whoever was on the other line.

Feeling dejected, Bambi didn't make her presence known and sneaked to her room. She entered her room and closed the door, but her mother's cries could still be heard. Bambi made her way to her bed and lied down. She needed to clear her head. Her naps never lasted long or really helped, but they helped her escape the cruelty of the world for a while. No longer being able to keep the tears in, she released them. Crying herself to sleep while listening to her mother's sobs.

Josh took a deep breath and knocked on the door in front of him. He had finally decided to let his father know how he was feeling. He wanted his father to know what his real dreams were, even if they didn't include the company. It didn't take long for him to get a reply. "Come in!"

His father placed the papers in his hand down, giving Josh his full attention. "Yes?" Josh took a seat in one of the office chairs and swallowed. "There's something I want to talk to you about." His father quirked in eyebrow and waited for him to speak.

Josh cleared his throat and sat up straighter. "The school year is coming close to an end," His father nodded "Yes. I'm aware of that." Josh closed his eyes, trying to find his previous courage "And, I've just been thinking of some things, lately. I know you want me to run the company, but…" His father released an annoyed breath "Josh, just get to the point."

He nodded and tried to focus on the painting behind his father. "I don't want to. I just don't have it in me, it's not

208

my passion." His father sat back in his chair and rested his hands under his chin. "And, what *is* your passion." He asked sarcastically.

"I-I'm thinking of pursuing football. There's going to be some college scouts from RoseOak University at the game next week. And, I think I have a good chance of being scouted. If not, I'm just going to play at Blueshores or Harlington."

Josh watched his father's lips turn up into a smile. He felt himself returning the smile, until his father began to laugh. Josh's smile slowly vanished and he prepared himself for the discouraging rant he was about to receive.

"Football?" His father's hands slammed down onto the desk "Football?! You want to give up the promise of wealth and stability, for football?! And, for what?! The hope that you *might* get drafted?" With a scoff, his father continued his verbal assault. "Wake up! This is real life, not some stupid fairy tale. You've got to make *real* decisions with *real* goals that will take you far." His father fixed his tie and waved his hand. "You're dismissed."

Josh watched his father's attention shift back to his papers. It angered him that his father was just going to dismiss everything he had said as if it was nothing. Before he knew it, he was shouting. "Do you know how it feels to *never* have your father ask how your day was or even care?! The only time you talk to me is when it involves your stupid business! I'm your son! Don't you care about me! You're the reason I grew up without a mom! Football is my passion and I'm really good at it! You would know that if you came to any of my games! This expression of *tough love* isn't going to do anything, but drive me away!"

Josh's chest was heaving up and down. His heart was exhilarating, pounding against his chest. It felt relieving to finally get what was on his chest out. Now, he could only hope that he was able to get through to his father.

A pair of blank eyes stared back at Josh. "Then, leave."

Josh froze and watched his father in disbelief. It had took him forever to build up the courage to express himself to his father. And, his father still proved to be the cold-emotionless person Josh knew him to be. Dropping his head, Josh chuckled humorlessly.

He blinked away the tears in his eyes and placed on a grin to hide his emotions "I just might do that." He said, responding to his father's earlier comment. He then stood up and took long strides to the door. He opened it whilst turning to look back at his father. "You, know? I now understand why she left you. You don't care about anyone, but yourself."

With that being said, Josh exited his father's office, slamming the door. He no longer cared what the consequences would be. Years and years, he would tell himself that his father wasn't truly cruel. All they needed was communication. But, even that failed him. The conversation with his father was all the conversation Josh needed, though. There was going to be no more trying to please his father. He had made his true feelings clear. So, Josh was going to do the same. It was time he start trying to make himself happy. Because in the end, he was the only person he had.

Smoke filled the room, but after a couple days Courtney had gotten used to it. The basement they were in was filthy and putrid. It belonged to one of Tatum's friends and many students used it as an escape. Courtney being one of them. Teens were crowded around the small space. The sound of glass breaking made Tatum's friend curse and rush off. Courtney didn't budge from her spot on the dingy couch. She took in her surroundings, realizing this is what her life had become. Drugs, Alcohol, and sex. Those were the attributes you had to be willing to comply with in order to fit into this world.

Courtney hadn't know that when she had signed the contract. It had left her emotionless and worst of all soulless. The fun she had made up for that, though. The fight between her and Bambi wasn't really a necessity. More like a fuel to keep the fire inside her burning. Courtney had never felt so alive, yet dead at the same time. It was like she no longer had control of herself anymore.

Tatum finished the conversation with the guy he was talking to and made his way over to her. He fell down onto the couch and placed his arm over her shoulders. "Dean said he's in. We just have to say when." Courtney sighed and ran her hand through her hair. Everything was moving too fast and she was starting to second-guess the plan. A lot of people were starting to get involved and it was no telling how far things would go. Not to mention, the trouble they could face. She decided to voice her worries with Tatum.

"I think we're taking things too far. We could get into a lot of trouble from this.

"Trust me. Even if things get out of control, they're not going to snitch. Not with all the dirt we've got on them, thanks to you. I can't believe all of them were pretending to be perfect, when they're just as bad as the rest of us. Don't worry they're going to get what they deserve."

"But-"

"I hope you're not having second thoughts Courtney. We're in this too deep. *All* of us." His voice was calm, but his eyes made the warning clear. "Besides, don't forget why this all happened in the first place. Bambi took your boyfriend and best friend. She tries to act all prissy when in all reality she's just a slut seeking attention. She probably became friends with you just to get at Josh and now she's using Amber to get to Ace. Pathetic. I don't see what everyone sees in them anyway. I play football just as good, if not better. But, because I don't live in SpringMeadows, I'm not good enough? Please. I'm ten times…."

Tatum's voice trailed off as Courtney ignored Tatum's obvious jealousy of his friends and leaned back against the couch. Tatum was right. They were already in too deep. She couldn't go back that would be allowing Bambi to win and she wasn't going to allow that to happen.

"Enough of that. Here. You need to relax." Courtney was brought out of her thought by Tatum. He held a red cup out to her. Its substances was unknown, but that didn't stop her from taking it. The usual burning feeling occurred. A feeling that would have made the old her recoil, but things had changed. It had turned into a feeling she craved for every day after school. If she decided to go. Alcohol was the acid to her dying rose. She didn't care what it was doing to her. Besides, water was just too boring. She took another swing from the cup and closed her eyes. *Who needs a soul when you've got other things to satisfy you?*

A little bit of kindness,

And a little bit of forgiveness,

The ingredients to a peaceful life,

Forgiveness does not dim the past,

But it does enlighten your future.

CHAPTER TWELVE

Forgiveness

The day was almost over. Once again, Courtney had not shown up to the farm. Making everyone's work twice as hard. Amber couldn't lie and say she didn't miss Courtney. They had been best friends since the ninth grade. It was always the two of them against everyone else in school. They were always there for one another. Every meltdown, tear, and heartbreak.

Amber could barely recognize Courtney, now. The new her dark and deceitful. Things the old Courtney was not. She was certain her friend was going through a very rough time. Only hoping she conquered whatever demons she was battling, before they took over her completely.

Amber couldn't focus on Courtney's problems, though. She had a couple demons of her own she was battling. Constantly, she would remind herself that she would get over her addiction. She could stop whenever she wanted too. She was fine. In all reality, she knew it was going to be easier said than done to fight this battle. With her parents putting too much pressure on her, school expecting so much, and the rising drama with Courtney. She didn't know what she was going to do. There sure wasn't anytime for her to try fighting an addiction. She was going to need the pills more than ever.

Amber was suddenly pulled out of her thoughts. Bambi and Josh both appeared by her sides, wearing mischievous grins. She frowned and crossed her arms, skeptically "What's going on?" Bambi and Josh nodded to one another and each grabbed one of her arms. "Come with us." They then proceeded to drag her along with them. Amber's frown grew deeper and she began to struggle in their grips. "What are you guys doing? Let go of me. You two are so childish! I'm telling Mr. Jones!" They released her upon her last threat.

Amber turned around to face them with a scowl and her hands placed on her hips. "What's going on?!" Josh inclined his head "Why don't you turn around and find out." Bambi bit her lip to keep from smiling. Cautiously, Amber turned around. Her scowl immediately began to fade away by what she was looking at.

It was beautiful. The sky that she had always known as blue had been painted a different color. Orange, Purple and Pink meshed together to form a beautiful work of art. The setting sun reflected off of the lake. A picnic was set up not too far from it.

She heard Bambi giggle from behind her and turned around. Her and Josh were taking steps backwards, the mischievous grins still on their faces. Bambi giggled again and spoke, teasingly "Hope you guys enjoy yourselves." The two of them then took off running from the way they had come.

Amber's eyebrows furrowed. She was confused by Bambi's comment, not seeing anyone else. Not a moment later, someone stepped from behind one of the trees. It was Ace. He was still dressed in his volunteer attire, but seemed to have cleaned up a bit. Amber wished she had been given the chance to do so, also. He held a rose in his hand and slowly made his way over to her.

Ace stopped when they were only inches apart and held the rose out to her. "Here. I'm sorry it took so long." Amber took the rose from his hand and looked into his eyes. Many times she had found herself falling into a trance, because of them. When she felt it beginning to happen, she blinked and broke eye contact. The moment was starting to become too overwhelming for her. Too many things were happening that were out of her control.

She sighed and let her hand holding the rose drop. "Ace…" He shook his head, taking her hands in his. "No. No more running away. It's only going to make things worse. You and I made a decision to breakup. A decision that wasn't ours. I still have feelings for you and I know they're not going to go away easily. In the beginning, I didn't fight for you. I'm willing to do that, now. But, only if I know I'm not alone in this."

Amber took a deep breath and blinked away her tears. She swallowed before speaking "Ace, you know I miss what we had. But, you and I both know how hard it was. We're both too different. We come from different worlds and live different lives. So, how are we supposed to make this work? When everyone else is so against us being together." The sadness in her voice was hard to miss.

He took in a deep breath "One of the biggest problems in our relationship was worrying about everyone else and moving too fast. We both have our lives ahead of us. But, it is *our* lives and we should choose whatever is going to make us happy. If we are what make each other happy, why fight it? If we want things to work we have to forget about everyone else and think of ourselves. Will take things slow and see where life takes us. Our lives are just starting, Amber."

Amber played his words over and over in her head. They had gotten to her. It felt relieving having Ace back in her life. He was as much as her support system as she was his. Without him, things had seemed to only get harder. She prayed they lasted. Letting her walls down, Amber allowed a tear to fall from her eye and smiled "I missed you"

That was all the signal Ace needed to pull her into his arms. Ace's embraces were always warm and comforting. She always felt safe in them. He helped ease her stress and her worries would fade away. As cliché as it was, nothing else mattered being in Ace's arms other than her happiness. Ace was Amber's first addiction. Her first stress reliever. They were similar in leaving her craving more. Their differences were one of them didn't fade away after a while.

Bambi snapped a picture from her camera. "Got, them!" She held the camera to her chest and sighed. "They're so good for one another." Josh had to agree. He glanced at his watch and spoke up "We should give them some privacy and start heading back to the farm" Bambi nodded and the two of them began to walk.

A comfortable silence fell on them, until Bambi broke it. "You, know? I can't lie. Watching Ace and Amber sort of makes me wish I had someone who cares about me that much" Josh felt the same way, but wasn't going to voice his thoughts. His problems at home were meant to stay at home. There was still something else on his mind.

Something that had been on his mind since the two of them had begun planning the setup for Ace and Amber. He battled with himself mentally, before he finally gained the courage to speak. "Hey, Bambi." She twisted her head to look at him. "Yeah?" He stopped and she copied his actions. Her eyes searched his face and she squinted her eyebrows in worry. "Josh?" She took a step closer to his frozen frame "Are you okay?" He snapped out of fear and nodded.

"Y-Yeah. Um, I just wanted to ask you something. If you don't mind." Bambi's worry was replaced with easiness. Her beaming smile made him both relaxed and nervous. He swallowed and tried to focus on other things. "Well...You

know…I was wondering if…maybe…you and I…could…"
Bambi nodded on for him to continue, but he was
interrupted.

"I've been looking everywhere for you!"

The two of them both snapped their neck in the
direction of where the voice had come from. Madison stood
a couple feet away from them with her arms crossed. She
tapped her foot and squinted her eyes at the both of them.
Her eyes switched back and forward between the two of
them. By Josh's nervousness and Bambi's obliviousness she
could tell what was going on. *You just make this too easy.*

Standing up straight, Madison focused her attention
on Bambi. "Old Man Jones wants us to make a delivery for
him. He said it's not too far from here, so he said we can
walk. Something about you needing the exercise or
something like that." The last comment had been a lie and
was made to taunt Bambi. Which it did by the way she
pulled at her shirt. Josh frowned at the situation "Well, I
think if anyone needs the exercise it would be you, Madison.
The guys and I were just talking about it. Something about

you losing your figure or something like that." Josh said, reversing Madison's taunt back at her.

Josh's comment was just as hurtful as hers had been to Bambi. Except Josh's comment would cause more damage to Madison than her comment would to Bambi. Meaning she would only retaliate harsher to the person she believed was responsible for her grief. Bambi.

"Whatever. No one was talking to you Josh. And, you!" she sent a sinister look to Bambi "This isn't over. Hurry up, because I'm not going to be late so you can just flirt with other people's boyfriend." Madison's words came up in snarls, making Bambi flinch. She opened her mouth to speak, but the other girl had already turned around and stomped off.

Bambi whirled around to face Josh "What was that?"

"I was defending you. Madison's just jealous. Don't listen to her." Josh said placing a hand on her shoulder. She snatched away from him and continued to shout "Still! You had no right stepping in! All you've done is make things worse! So, next time just mind your own business!" Josh frowned "So, I'm just supposed to mind my own business when you're getting ridiculed for things you didn't do and don't deserve."

"Yes! I'm used to things like this happening. It's been like this since the ninth grade and you defending me isn't going to stop it! Fighting fire with fire isn't going to do anything, but create a bigger fire! So, just drop it!"

She twisted around and began to walk away, but Josh next words made her freeze. "I can see why people bully you, now! All you do is let people walk all over you. Maybe, Madison was right! Maybe, you do all this for attention! If you would just grow some balls and stop playing the victim, maybe you'd be able to stand up for yourself!"

Bambi turned around to face him. The expression on her face, instantly made him regret his words. Her face was pulled into a frown. This was the angriest Josh had seen Bambi. Even though she was frowning, tears continued to roll down her face. She used her arms to wipe her face and chuckled, humorlessly. "Yeah. I may be weak in everyone's

eyes just, because I don't use my words or fists to fight back.
It shouldn't matter that I know how it feels to be hurt and
wouldn't want anyone else to experience it. But, you know
what? My mother always told me this, another thing you can
label me *weak* for. It takes a bigger person to walk away like
from things like that without lashing out. Just like I'm going
to do right now."

Josh wanted to say something. Something that
would make her feel better and help her forget his earlier
words, but he couldn't think of anything. Like everyone else,
he had attacked Bambi for nothing. Taking out his own
feelings on her. Like everyone else, he had proven why there
was a separation such as *Popular* and *Outsiders*.

Madison stood by a couple bags whilst holding her
own. Bambi kept her eyes casted down, as she grew closer to
her. "About time." Madison spoke, once she was close
enough. Bambi ignored her and reached for the others bags.
"Were you crying?" Bambi ignored her question and wiped

her cheeks "Just leave me alone." She picked up the bags and began walking. Feeling eyes on her, she turned around. Madison didn't make a move from the spot she was in. The look she was giving Bambi confused her. It was strange and indescribable. "What?" Madison snapped out of her daze and glared. "Nothing. Come on. We're already running late because of you."

A couple minutes had passed and Bambi was growing tired. "Any idea who's house were going to, anyway?" Madison continued to look forward and released a huff "Look. I'm not here to make conversation with you, so please just keep that mouth of yours shut. Might be hard, seeing as though you've never been able to do so in the past."

Bambi scowled and crossed her arms. She was getting sick of Madison's harsh treatment to her. Josh might not have worded things correctly, but he was right. It was time she stop letting people walk all over her. She took an abrupt stop and turned to look at the other girl. "Madison when are you going to let what happened go. It was a long time ago and I've apologized a thousand times."

Madison raised an eyebrow and looked Bambi over. A smirk made its way to her lips, as she placed her hands on her hips. She chuckled humorlessly "Was that supposed to be another one of your silly apologies?" Her smirk was replaced with a sneer "I already told you. I'm not stopping until you've felt my pain. I'm not stopping until you stop playing the victim. Remember there was a time when you and I were just a like."

Bambi frowned and took a step closer to her "You know that's a lie, Madison. Those are *very* different scenarios. You and I are nothing a like." Madison crossed her arms and took a step back "You sure about that? In less than a couple of weeks, you've managed to sabotage one girl's relationship and friendship. All so you could have a couple friends." She finished with a pout.

Her finger was placed by her lip in thought. "Wait, you are right. We are nothing alike. I'd say you're worst."

When Bambi's face faltered, Madison knew she had won the battle. She turned about and took her sunglasses from her head, placing them on. Bambi kept quiet the rest of the walk, trailing behind Madison. She tried not to let her words affect her, but they continued to play back in her mind. The logical piece of her mind ignored Madison, but the emotional one held onto and believed everything she had said.

By the look on her face, Madison could tell Bambi was also surprised. Neither one of them had been expecting Ms. Clover to open the door when they arrived. They were now in her kitchen, as they helped her place away the stuff. Madison tried to avoid eye contact as much as she could. In only a matter of months, Ms. Clover had drastically changed. She no longer resembled the sweet and preppy counselor they remembered. Her appearance was unkempt and she looked as if she hadn't been getting any sleep. Madison wondered what had happened to the lady. The older woman had also been acting a little resistant to her. She couldn't stand Ms. Clover's over happiness in the past, but she would prefer it over this dark and lifeless one.

Once they were finished, Ms. Clover spoke. "Well, that's the last of it. Thank you girls for helping me." Bambi spoke up, giving her a sympathetic smile. Madison was happy, she wasn't the only one that felt bad for the woman. "Its fine, Ms. Clover. I know what happened. Are you okay?"

Madison's eyebrow's knitted together. What had Bambi heard? And why hadn't she heard of it also? Ms. Clover's smile fell for a moment. The next one was forced. She took a seat in one of the kitchen table chairs and sighed "I'm as good as any mother would be after losing their child?" She then placed on another forced smile. "It's alright, though. Peyton might be gone, but he'll never be forgotten."

Swallowing, Madison stuttered out "H-How did he die?"

The smile on Ms. Clover's face slowly faded. The look she gave Madison sent chills up her spine. It was an accusing look. *This* Ms. Clover didn't look depressed. She looked furious. "He committed suicide. He was being bullied at school. Kids picked on him for the way he dressed. Peyton always liked dressing up nice. No matter what it was for. School, Church, it didn't matter. I loved him for it, but it was obvious they didn't. They killed him out of their own self-hate." Even, though Ms. Clover wore a frown, she spoke calmly.

Madison couldn't believe what she was hearing. Her mind drifted back to past memories. Memories she now wished she could erase. She shook her head clear of those thoughts. "Do you know that for sure? I mean, there could have been lots of reasons he decided to kill himself. Maybe his home life was bad."

Bambi frowned from her position of consoling Ms. Clover. She shook her head, disapprovingly "Madison…" She was interrupted by Ms. Clover. Madison's comment had struck a nerve in Ms. Clover and the older woman didn't hold back her fury as she spoke.

"I loved my son and showed him that love every chance I got! He was not unhappy at home! That wasn't the problem! The problem was him going to that damn school full of kids who have nothing better to do than ruin others' lives. Peyton was a good kid! He didn't deserve any of that! I may have not known he was getting bullied, but I was a damn good mother and you will not take that away from me!"

Growing tired from yelling, Ms. Clover placed her hand to her chest. Her body shook with the sob that wanted to be released. Bambi rubbed her back, sympathetically. Ms. Clover took a deep breath, calming herself down and spoke softly "My only mistake was not seeing that he was unhappy. I'm a school counselor! My job is to make sure students are okay. To be there when they needed me. I couldn't even do that for my own son" she chuckled, humorlessly. Tears surfacing in her eyes "The one person that needed me the most was coming home with me every day. But, I was too wrapped up in my own world to see he was dying right in front of me."

Ms. Clover sniffled and wiped her face. She stood up and walked toward one of the kitchen draws. "I had been meaning to give this to you, but I never got around to it…." She opened the draw and pulled an envelope out. "He left a note." She said, holding it out to Bambi.

Both girls were shocked. With shaking hands, Bambi reached out to take the letter. She could barely get her words out "P-Peyton?" Ms. Clover nodded, a sad smile had taken over her face. "Yes. Apparently, he knew you. He left a couple of notes the day he…." She cleared her throat. "Yours was one of them."

"B-But, we only spoke once. I don't understand. Why would he write me a letter?"

"All it takes is one time, to make a big impact in others' lives."

It was Bambi's turn to get emotional. She shook her head in grief "I'm so sorry this had to happen to you, Ms. Clover."

The older woman shook her head. "It's okay. I forgive them." Her eyes shifted to Madison for a second, but Bambi had managed to catch it. "All of them."

Not wanting to hear anymore, Madison turned on her heels dashing out of the kitchen. Bambi twisted around and called out to the girl "Madison!"

"Go." Bambi faced Ms. Clover whose eyes were focused on a picture of Peyton "That girl…." She trailed off, taking a deep breath and focusing her eyes back on Bambi "….needs help more than anyone else."

Bambi nodded and turned around, running after the girl. Ms. Clover placed a hand to her forehead, finally letting the tears out. "Why? Why him? Why *my* son?" Slowly, she sank to the ground, as the sobs punched through her body.

"Madison! Madison!" Bambi yelled out, trying to get the other girl to stop. She didn't, so she just increased her pace. Eventually catching up to the other girl and grabbing her arm. "Stop."

Madison yanked her arm away "Don't touch me!" Bambi sighed. She looked into her eyes and was taken back. For the first time, Madison actually looked scared. It was then, Bambi truly understood the girl. She was just scared and Bambi felt sorry for her. "Madison, I understand that-"

Madison laughed. It sounded painful. "No, you don't! You don't understand anything! Ms. Clover's son is gone! She didn't deserve that!"

Bambi nodded "You're right. She didn't deserve any of that. No one does." Madison rolled her eyes "Whatever, I can't think about everyone else. All I know is some lady's son is dead. A lady who never hurt anyone. And I might be one of the people that contributed to it."

Bambi reached her hand out to her "Madison…" She stepped away from her and shook her head. "No, leave me alone." She then turned around to walk away.

Bambi caught her arm and pulled her back. "No. We need to talk or else you're going to continue destroying people's lives, including your own. You never listen to me, but today I'm going to force you. It's time you know the truth about that day. After that, if you still hate me I don't know what more I can do. But, you need to know the truth!"

Six years ago

Bambi and Laura waited in front of the movie theater. Their mothers had dropped them off and they had already bought their tickets. The only thing left was Madison. The other girl was supposed to have met them there, but she was now running twelve minutes late.

Laura huffed and stomped her feet "Ugh! Where is she?! You said she was going to be here." It was Laura's birthday. She was new to the town, only being there for a couple of months. For a long time, it had just been Madison and Bambi, but the two of them was happy to have a new friend. Bambi had been a little reluctant to the girl, but Madison had convinced her to accept her

"Let's just go inside, before we miss it! Madison can just join us whenever she comes." Bambi tried not to roll her eyes at the bratty girl. "Just wait, she'll be here. She probably had an emergency." Laura rolled her eyes "Fine."

Just then, Bambi's phone beeped. She opened the little flip phone and read over the text message she had received.

911 was "code" for her parents fighting. Madison's parents were going through a nasty divorce and she wasn't

taking it well. Apparently, Madison's father wasn't content with just Madison's mother. Bambi was more upset with the fact of being stuck with Laura. She sent Madison a text saying it was okay.

Bambi looked up to face Laura and delivered the message. She looked from Bambi to the phone "So? Is she coming?" Bambi sighed and shook her head "No. Something came up. She can't make it."

Laura huffed "Unbelievable. Something came up? And, it just so happens to be on my birthday?"

The spoiled girl frowned, but then a smile took over her face. She smiled and face palmed "Of course! I know what the problem really is?" Bambi's eyes widened "You, do?" She was shocked. They hadn't known the girl that long, so why would Madison tell her what was going on.

Laura flipped her hair over her shoulders "Duh. It's obvious. Madison keeps bailing on us, because she doesn't fit in. She probably just jealous, because we have nice things and dress nice. While she looks...well, you've seen her." Laura then proceeded to break out into a fit of giggles.

Bambi hated the girl's annoying laugh, but what she hated most was the way she had spoken of Madison. "Shut up! You don't know what you're talking about. Madison is the sweetest person you'll ever meet. She's just going through family problems right now. How would you feel if your parents were getting a divorce? She's not jealous of anyone. You're just a brat who thinks the world revolves around her and I don't want to be friends with someone like you."

Laura scowled "Fine! Who needs loser friends like you guys! You guys will just ruin my image anyway."

Bambi ignored the girl, texting her mom to pick her up. She didn't need to be friends with someone like Laura and neither did Madison. It had always been the two of them against everyone else and they were fine just like that.

The Next Day

Bambi had overslept and missed the bus, so her mother had to drop her off. She had been sending Madison text messaged all morning, but she hadn't responded to any of them. As, she neared her locker loud laughter could be heard. Bambi followed the noise and was confused to see a bunch of people crowded around her and Madison's lockers.

The closer she got, the angrier she became. Madison was cowering, as Laura and a couple other girls surrounded her. They were all laughing, but nothing they were doing looked funny.

"I heard your parents are getting a divorce, because your dad's an alcoholic."

"I heard he's a gambler and spent all their money."

"Well, that'll explain her clothes."

The girls laughed and that's when Bambi noticed the tears and Madison's eyes. She knew she had to help her best friend and quickly pushed her way through the crowd. She stood in front of Madison, blocking her from Laura and the others. "Leave her alone, Laura!"

The other girl crossed her arms and took a step closer, invading Bambi's space. "Or what? I can't believe you're defending her. You shouldn't even be hanging out *with someone like her. Look at her, she's never at school, always comes to school wearing the same things, and-"*

Before, she could say another insult. Bambi pushed the girl with all her strength. Laura fell and her friends rushed to help her. She pushed all of their hands off her and glared at Bambi. "I don't know why you're so angry, Bambi. You're the one who told me in the first place."

Bambi froze.

Madison was in disbelief "W-What?"

Laura smirked and tilted her head "Oh. You didn't know? Yep, little miss Bambi told me all about your parent's divorce. Guess she's not as good as a friend like you thought."

Bambi whirled around and "Madison...I.."

The other girl shook her head and ran away crying. Bambi called out to her, but she didn't stop. She gave Laura and her friends a glare and took off after her best friend.

Bambi found Madison crying under one of the staircases. She sat down next to her and tried rubbing her back. She only snatched away from her "Move. D-Don't touch me. You're an h-horrible friend."

A tear slipped from Bambi's eye seeing her friends like this. "Madison, I'm sorry. I didn't mean to tell her, I swear. Listen, we-"

"No!"

Madison jumped up "I don't want to hear anything you have to say. You're supposed to be my best friend and you betray me for a girl we barely know! I was there for you when your mom would work long hours and you would cry, because you thought she didn't love you. But, do you hear me blabbing your business to the school. No, because I'm a good friend and it's obvious you're not."

It was Bambi's turn to get upset "I said I made a mistake, okay! If you were my friend, you would understand and try to work things out. Not throw our whole friendship away, because of one small incident!"

Madison frowned "One small incident that the whole school now knows about! Don't you understand, Bambi? I'm going to be the one bullied, not you. It's bad enough I have to go home and listen to my parents fight every day. Now, this stupid divorce is going to follow me everywhere I go. I'm going to be known as the daughter of the man who couldn't stay faithful to his wife. Do you know how embarrassing that is?!"

Madison sighed "Look, I have enough problems to deal with and you just only added on a lot more. I don't think we should be best friends anymore. For now on, stay away from me."

With that being said, Madison turned to walk away. Tears rushed down Bambi's eyes and she angrily rubbed them away. "Fine...Who needs you....I don't want to be friends with you either...I don't need you...I don't need anybody" her voice cracked at the end, as she fell into a sob.

She was losing one of the most important people in her life. Little did Bambi know, that would be the last time she saw **that** Madison. Her best friend was gone.

After, that day. Laura and her friends continued to bully and taunt Madison. It was like this all the way to eight grade. They would always come up with something to mess with or accuse the other girl about. Bambi just kept her distance and minded her own business. There would be times where she wanted to help Madison, but then she would remember her words. **Stay away.** *So, Bambi did. She stayed away and watched from a distance as her best friend endured hell from their classmates. Both she and Madison had no one. Without each other, they were loners. Everyone knew of them, which in a way made them popular. But, nonetheless. They were still outsiders and nothing was going to change that.*

By the time, they had made it to High School. Laura had been shipped off to military school for her behavior. This had made Bambi happy. With Laura gone meant she could start over and have a brand new start. She was looking forward to making friends her freshmen year, but that was quickly shut down by Madison.

The first day of school, Bambi had barely recognize her. The nerdy Madison was gone, replaced by a supermodel. Bambi had tried to reach out to her that day and apologize for abandoning her. Now, that she was older. She had realized how stupid that had been. Madison had not accepted her apology, though. In fact, she laughed at it.

She claimed to be over it. Bambi felt relieved and now looked forward to them going back to the way things were. That was until, the day continued to go on and she was able to witness just how much Madison had changed. The victim had become the bully and she made sure Bambi was her main target. Every time Bambi or someone would ask her why she would say one word. Payback.

Everyone thought Madison was going a bit overboard, but said nothing. No one could believe someone like Bambi could do anything bad. Bambi and Madison knew the truth, though. So, Madison continued to bully her and Bambi let her. Whereas Madison saw it as justified payback, Bambi saw it as her rightful punishment. And through every punishment, she would hope that maybe somehow the old Madison would come back. But, maybe that was too much to hope for.

Present Day

Tears were in Bambi's eyes. She was finally able to tell Madison the truth about that day "So, for the last time. *I'm sorry, Madison.*" The sorrow could be heard in her apology.

Madison's face was now drenched in tears and she used her arm to wipe her face. She then wrapped her arms around herself "No, I don't believe you. You did all of that on purpose. You were never my friend."

"I was your friend and would still be if you let me! Madison, I didn't do any of that stuff on purpose and you have to believe me! What I just told you is the truth! You were my best friend! I would never try to purposely hurt you and I'm sorry that you had to go through what you did, because of me. I'm sorry. Please, let's put this all behind us." Bambi said, holding her hand out.

Madison's eyes were focused on the ground. She thought over Bambi's words. Maybe, it was time to put things behind them. It had been six years and since then both of their lives had been in chaos. She raised her head and reached her hand out towards Bambi's. Another thought then crossed her mind. None of this would be happening if it had not been for Bambi.

Bambi watched as the old Madison disappeared once again. Madison folded her arms together and looked Bambi over. "Nice try." She sneered and turned around. Bambi didn't even bother calling out to her that time. It was no use. She was convinced the old Madison was gone for good.

"Bambi,"

She whirled around, spotting Ms. Clover watching her from the porch. *Had she been watching the whole time?* Ms. Clover gave her a small smile and motioned inside. "Come. I think there's a couple important things we need to talk about." Bambi looked over her shoulder in the direction of Madison's disappearing figure, before nodding her head and making her way toward Ms. Clover.

Ms. Clover took a seat at the dining room table and Bambi sat across from her. This time she actually took a look around the place. It had an antique, vintage theme going on. Pictures of Peyton covered the walls. Looking at the pictures, you would think Peyton was a happy kid. And, from the amount of pictures you could tell Ms. Clover loved her son. *I guess that's why no one saw it coming?*

"Would you like something to drink?"

Bambi snapped out of her thoughts and shook her head at Ms. Clover's question. "No, thanks." Ms. Clover didn't respond and instead continued to silently watch her. Bambi tried to hide her growing discomfort by focusing her attention on her fidgeting fingers.

"You're just like him."

Bambi lifted her head and furrowed her eyebrows. She followed Ms. Clover's gaze to a picture of Peyton. The older woman sighed "He was shy and quiet, just like you. Never liked for the attention to be on him. I had tried getting him to break out of his shell, but nothing ever worked. Sometimes, I would get angry at him for not acting like other

248

kids. Doing things *normal* teenagers do." She took a breath and smiled "If only I would have knew that the *normal* things weren't always the good things. Now, I'm without a son-" Ms. Clover's voice broke at the end and Bambi reached across the table to grab her hand.

"You don't have to do this, Ms. Clover." She only patted Bambi's hand and shook her head. "No. I need to. I didn't do things right the first time, but now I have a second chance." Bambi was confused by her statement, but allowed her to continue. "Peyton pretended to be happy, he forced himself to smile, and I fell for it all. A mother always feels as if she's doing the best when it comes to their child. Never would one contemplate that their child might be suicidal. I was one of them."

"There were so many signs. So many signs that I did not notice. Unexplainable injuries, destroyed electronics, missing things, nightmares, and failing grades." She ranted "I was never a mother to overbear my child about his grades, but from the time Peyton had entered the first grade, he had gotten nothing lower than a B. He gets here and is coming home with D's and F's."

"I would try to confront him on things, but he would always push me away. Sometimes, he'd even lash out. Yelling and shouting at me to just *leave him alone*. I wish I would have knew he was really talking to his bullies. Every day, he would get home from school and rush to his room. Shutting and locking the door. It was like a safe haven for him. I thought he was just being the average teen boy and just wanted space, so that's what I gave him. But, the more space I gave him, the closer he got to the edge, until he finally jumped off."

Bambi wondered if her mother could see the signs. There had been numerous times when Bambi would just push her mother away just like Peyton, not wanting to recall what was happening to her at school. Plus, she felt her mother had enough problems to deal with. Her being bullied would just add onto them.

Ms. Clover squeezed Bambi's hand gently, gaining her attention. "I know you're thinking of your own mother. And, I'm *begging* you, Bambi to tell her what's going on. For both you guys' sake. No child should ever deal with depression alone which leads to them taking their own life.

And, no mother should ever have to deal with losing their child. Especially, knowing that child took their own life as a result of being bullied."

"So, *please* talk to your mother, Bambi. Because it hurts. It really hurts…"

Bambi walked into her home, shutting the door behind her. Her mother was running late, so for a short while she would be alone. She didn't really mind it, though. Right now, she needed extra time to herself to grasp things. Too many things had happened today. Her arguments with both Josh and Madison, and the discussion with Ms. Clover.

Ms. Clover's words were weighing heavy on her mind. She wanted to tell her mother what was going on at school, but she was also scared. Mostly scared of what the outcome would be. Being seen as weak. Getting more backlash from the bullies. Her mother not really understanding or caring about what she was going through.

"You're just like him."

Bambi suddenly remembered something. Reaching into her back pocket, she pulled out the letter Ms. Clover had given her. It felt heavy in her hands. Bambi walked into the living room, taking a seat on one of the sofas. Her heart was pounding in her chest.

She had only spoken to Peyton once, yet he had left her a note. When she thought of Peyton, all she would see is the shy, well-dressed boy she had met in the field. The friend she had hoped to have. A child that was taken from their mother too soon. *I should have done something.*

Bambi could feel an anxiety attack coming on, but things were honestly getting too overwhelming. *How could I have not seen the signs?* Of all people, Bambi should have been able to see that Peyton was hanging on by a thin thread. But, like everyone else she had only been thinking of herself. All she saw was a chance at having a friend. Seeing Peyton as a profit first and not a person. Pushing away her emotions, Bambi finally got the courage to open the letter.

To, Bambi My First Friend,

Hi, this is Peyton. By the time you've gotten this, I should be dead. Honestly speaking, I probably shouldn't even be writing you a letter, right now. But, I can see you've found your cliff and I want to stop you from jumping off. It's much too late for me. I'm at the edge and it's starting to crumble. You were the first person at RoseOak to speak to me kindly. And, the only one to offer to be friends. I wish I would have met you sooner. Maybe, things would have turned out different. Unlike me, you've got a chance to turn things around. You're not at the edge, but you're close and I don't want you to get there. There's something special about you. You can't let them break you. Tell someone what's going on. Don't just deal with it on your own like me. Get help! Whatever you do, just don't give up. That day you helped me feel happy for once at school. It wasn't enough to stop me, but like I said, I was too far gone. But think of all the other kids you can help that are like us. They need someone like you. You might not see it Bambi, but you're going to make a difference. And, wherever I am, I'll be watching and encouraging you along the way.

Peyton

By the time Bambi was finished with the letter, her faced was covered in tears. Before she could get her thoughts together, she could hear the front door being opened.

"Bambi! I'm home!"

She heard her mother placed her keys down and shuffle around in the kitchen. Bambi continued to cry, now covering her mouth. It must have not muffled the sounds that much. *"Bambi? Is that you? Are you in the living room?"*

She didn't respond and soon her mother's footsteps could be heard. She walked into the living room, calling out to her *"Bambi, didn't you hear me calling you?"* Still not getting a response, her mother came closer to her.

"Bambi-" She paused, once she was able to see the state her daughter was in. Her mother kneeled in front of her, pushing her hair away from her face. She held her cheeks, stroking them with her thumb "Sweetheart, what's wrong?" Bambi could no longer hold the sobs in and rushed into her mother's arms.

"Mom...I need help. Please..."

Her mother didn't respond, but her arms tightened around her. She stroked her back and kissed her forehead. "It's okay, baby. I got you. You're going to be okay. We're going to get you through this together, okay?" Bambi nodded, burying her head into her mother's chest.

A grave for me,

And a grave for you,

That's what revenge can do,

No one ever wins in revenge,

Because pain is never forgoten,

So the grudge never ends.

CHAPTER THIRTEEN

Revenge

"You look so beautiful." Bambi's mom gushed. Bambi grimaced at her mother's camera flash, as she took *another* picture. "Mom…please. No more." She begged. After the ninth picture, Bambi had begun to lose count and patience. Tonight was the event every girl had been waiting for-Prom.

Bambi had gotten ready and was now waiting on the rest of the group to show up. Which consisted of Ace, Amber, and Josh. The two of them hadn't spoken since their argument at the farm and Bambi prayed things wouldn't be awkward between them.

Another flash caused Bambi to snap out of her thoughts. "Mom!" she exclaimed, rubbing at her eyes. "No more pictures!" Her mother rolled her eyes, but listened to her wishes and placed the camera away. She stared at Bambi for a moment with a smile on her face, before walking up to her, pulling her into a hug.

Bambi groaned and laughed, hugging her mother back. "Okay, mom. I can't breathe." Bambi wheezed out. Her mother released her, but still held her at arm's length. She gave Bambi a serious look and spoke. "I want you to have fun tonight, okay?" Bambi nodded with a roll of her eyes. "I will." Her mother looked her over again and as expected, pulled her into another hug. "I'm *so* happy for you."

Bambi understood her mother's over happiness, so she didn't get annoyed. A week ago, her mother had taken her to a mental health center to help with her depression. Since, she wasn't as bad as she was before. Her mother and therapist agreed with her wish to start the program after the school year was finished.

The doorbell rang and her mother quickly released her, taking fast steps to the door. She gave Bambi an overexcited smile then opened the door. Her mother released a gasp and beckoned her friends to come in.

"Aww! You guys just look so cute. I need pictures!" From behind her mother, Bambi's head fell with exasperation. "I promise I won't go overboard." Bambi sighed, as another round of taking pictures began.

Together, the four of them entered the gym where the prom was being held. They all looked around in awe, actually impressed with the prom's decorations. A fast song was playing and teens surrounded the dance floor with their dates. The car ride hadn't been so awkward for the most part. Bambi conversed with Amber, while Josh did the same with Ace. She knew they could since the obvious tension between her and Josh, but thankfully they hadn't said anything.

Ace suddenly turned to Amber and leaned to whisper in her ear. "Let's dance." Amber giggled and nodded. She smiled small and waved at Bambi, letting Ace lead her to the dance floor. Bambi wanting to beg Amber not to leave her with Josh, but her friend was happy and seemed relaxed. Which was a rare thing. Plus, her and Ace had been through a lot and deserved to spend this night together happy. Bambi tried distracting herself by looking around the cafeteria. Not wanting to make eye contact with Josh.

She smiled and laughed to herself, watching Ace and Amber. They both had two left feet and couldn't dance to save their lives. That didn't stop them, though. They were in their own little world, as they tried to *badly* out dance one another.

"Hey."

Bambi turned her head and looked up to see Josh looking down at her. His intense gaze made her somewhat nervous. She swallowed "Y-Yeah." His hand reached up to rub his neck-a bad habit of his. Bambi knew this was a sigh that he was nervous and was thankful she wasn't the only one feeling it. "Can we talk?" Bambi looked around, chewing on her lip, before nodding. "Sure."

He led them over to the snack table. Josh was the first to speak. "Look. I'm sorry, okay. I didn't mean to yell at you that day. Seeing you get put down by Madison had struck a nerve in me. I know what it feels like to get bullied by those that think they have more power than you and having no one to stand up for you. I didn't want you to go through that. I didn't want you to feel alone." Bambi nodded.

She should have knew from the start why Josh had gotten upset. The two of them have discussed the relationship he and his dad had numerous of times. It always bothered him to see someone being bullied, but he never does anything and regrets it every time. Actually knowing Bambi must have helped him gain the courage to finally say something.

"I know, Josh. It's okay. I shouldn't have gotten mad in the first place. It was childish. Let's go back to how things were, before the fight." Josh released a breath and looked away from her, causing Bambi's eyebrow's to furrow. *Why is he upset?*

She heard him mumble something and squinted her eyes "Huh?" He huffed and faced her again, grabbing her hands "I said, I don't want things to go back to the way they were, before" Bambi looked from their hands to him, shaking her head "I don't understand-"

His next sentence almost made her faint.

"I like you, okay." Bambi's eyes widened, as she felt her heart rate speed up. She fought hard to get her words out "Courtney…" Josh took a deep inhale and tightened his hold on her hands.

"What Courtney and I had was never serious. Fun. That's all it was. The both of us distracted each other from the problems in our lives, with one another. We used each other to run away from our issues rather than face them. Courtney caught me at a weak and vulnerable period. But, I'm ready to take my life serious and move forward. And, continuing that fast and reckless lifestyle with her would only stop that."

Bambi shook her head, overwhelmed with the whole thing. "I don't know, Josh. I-"

"Do you like me?" Bambi's head shot up at his question. She felt herself get butterflies in her stomach and her hands he was holding tingle. He waited for an answer, staring at her, as she thought his question over. *Did I like him?*

Bambi thought over all the time they had spent together. The talks they had. The moments when he would make her laugh and he would make her smile. Her nerves were all over the place and her thoughts jumbled. She had never felt this way about a boy. And, didn't even know she had been harboring these feelings, until Josh revealed his.

"Bambi?"

She snapped out of her thoughts and looked into his eyes. It was clear to her why she had never been able to do so, before. Things were different with Josh. With other boys, she would not make eye contact, because she didn't want to be notice. Whereas with Josh, she would look away wondering if he was looking at her and then steal a quick glance herself. She would always get caught, though. This would only cause Josh to smile. Which in return, caused her to smile. Bambi knew the answer to his question.

"No."

Abruptly, Josh's face fell and he released her hands, prepared to walk away. Bambi giggled and grabbed his hands, pulling him back towards her. "I was kidding," she teased, laughing. "I like you too." Josh still wore a displeased face and Bambi scowled. "Why are you mad? You're the one always telling me to loosen up and joke around."

Josh frowned "But, not about things like *that*. Your jokes aren't funny, they're brutal." Bambi laughed, but then began to get serious. "I like you, Josh. But, part of me is still nervous. I've never done anything like this, before." Bambi explained, feeling a little embarrassed. She didn't want him to think she was childish or naïve.

He did neither one of those things and only brought her hands up to his lips. He kissed her knuckles and grinned "Okay, well we'll take things slow, okay? There's no rush."

Bambi felt herself blush and looked away. Josh spoke up again, pulling her to him "Besides, this is new for me too, you know?" Bambi raised an eyebrow, waiting for him to elaborate "I've never been with a *good* girl." He taunted, causing Bambi to hit him.

Suddenly, the song playing changed to something slow. Couples who weren't dancing made their way to the dance floor and those who were calmed down. Bambi felt Josh leave her side, as he moved to stand in front of her. He held his hand out and bowed "May I have this dance?" Once again, Bambi felt herself blush and hurriedly took his hand to hide it.

Standing in a corner, Courtney glowered having seen the whole scene between Josh and Bambi. *He's never treated me like that.* Courtney looked Bambi over, wondering what Josh even saw in Bambi. Body wise, Courtney had Bambi beat any day. Without her pretty face, Bambi had nothing on Courtney. She heard Tatum scoff from beside her

"Of all people, Bambi chooses Josh." He laughed to himself "She could do better."

Courtney rolled her eyes. Hoping Tatum didn't have a crush on Bambi, also. "Like, who? You?" She said speaking on his last comment and scoffed. Tatum stood up from leaning on the wall and glared at her "Whatever. Tell me when you're ready to do the plan. Don't get chicken, either." Courtney only waved him off.

Her eyes roamed the gym and locked eyes with Amber. Courtney felt herself freeze, as her and her once best friend held eye contact. Amber was never supposed to get in the middle of any of this and Courtney was beginning to feel bad. She looked away, breaking eye contact. Only to look up again and be met with a different sight. Josh and Bambi had made their way over to them. They all began to joke around and Courtney felt her blood began to boil. Her guilt was now gone. Amber had chosen her side.

A body came to stand next to her and she turned, seeing Madison. Her appearance surprised Courtney. The beauty queen, cheerleader looked nothing like herself. None of her assets were on display and for once her face wasn't caked with makeup. *The top dog has lost her bark.* Courtney smirked and crossed her arms, leaning back against the wall. "Finally come to your senses and going to join us?" she taunted. Madison took a deep breath "Look. I know we haven't spoken since the party, but I know you're still going through with your plan."

Courtney shrugged "And?"

"And, I don't think you should. I was wrong for bullying Bambi for so long over something that happened a long time, ago. I was holding onto a stupid grudge, but I know better now. Bullying ruins people lives, okay? No one wins. Bad things happen. Things you can't change or take back. I'm not sure you want to do this, Courtney. I've been there. It's no coming back."

Courtney picked at her nails, not really paying attention to what Madison was saying. "Are you done with your little sob story?" She smirked and pushed off the wall "Why don't you go tell Bambi all of that. Maybe then you guys can be friends and everything will be all sunshine and lollipops!" Courtney exclaimed, mockingly.

Her smirk then drop, as she looked Madison over. "You honestly think you can change your look and put on this *good girl act*, and Bambi will want to be your friend, again. You've put her through hell since freshmen year. She'd be an idiot to want to be friends with you, again."

Madison took a step toward Courtney "Stop the plan." Courtney came closer to Madison, until their faces were inches apart. "Or, what?"

"You've lost your crown Madison. There's a new queen bee around here. But, this queen is ten times as wicked than you'll ever be. So take my advice. You don't want to get in my way or else you'll go down too." She threatened.

Madison released a breath, backing away from Courtney "We'll see about that."

Tatum appeared at Courtney side and whistled "What was that about? You guys looked ready to rip each other's heads off." Courtney took Tatum's cup from his hand, taking a sip. As expected, he had slipped some alcohol into it. "Looks like she's one of them." She sighed and flicked her hair over her shoulders "It's a shame, really. I was trying to give her the benefit of the doubt." She handed the cup back to Tatum and he frowned, noticing half of it was already gone "You're an alcoholic."

Courtney cut her eyes at him and began walking. He hastily followed after her. "Tell the guys to go ahead and put her in it, too." Tatum nodded and saluted her.

Courtney allowed her eyes to roam around the gym. Finding each one of her targets. They all seemed to be relaxed and enjoying themselves. Courtney smirked. Neither one of them were even aware of what she had planned for them. That only made things more exciting. "Time to show everyone who's boss around here."

Bambi pulled her eyes away from Josh, to focus on the woman on stage. They had stopped the music and were going to announce prom king and queen.

"And, the prom king and queen are....drum roll please," the woman opened the envelope and shouted through the microphone *"Ace Woods and Madison Jackson!"*

Both Bambi and Amber screamed along with the crowd, while Josh grinned wide, slapping Ace on the back. Ace pulled Amber into a kiss, making everyone cheer louder, before jogging to the stage. He stood by Madison and they both got their crowns placed on. Bambi locked eyes with Madison and was surprised to see the girl smile at her. Bambi recovered from her shock and returned the smile, giving her two thumbs up. Madison mouthed back 'thank you' and turned back toward the crowd.

Josh spoke from behind Bambi "Did Madison just smile and thank you?" Bambi shrugged, not understanding it herself. She wasn't going to spend too much time questioning it, though. The night was getting better and better, as time went by. Bambi knew this would be a day she never forgot.

And then, the lights went out.

"Attention, RoseOak students. One of your fellow peers speaking here. Sorry to interrupt, but before anymore lies continue, I think you all should know the TRUTH about the very people you all worship and seem to love so much!"

"The doors are locked!" Bambi heard a few people scream, panicking. She could recognize the voice that was obviously Courtney's. She, Amber, Ace, Josh, and Madison all shared a looked.

Suddenly the screen on stage, displaying the winners switched from their names to a pictures of Ace. Amber gasped and Bambi's eyes widened. A picture had been shot of Ace taking steroids from what looked like the locker rooms.

"Explains why he's the best!"

Courtney said then laughed. All eyes were on Ace, as he stood frozen on the stage. Before, he could react the screen switched, again.

Replacing Ace's picture was a picture of Amber. She was in the girl's bathroom, appearing to be taking some pills. Bambi faced forward, as all eyes shifted to her friend.

"RoseOak's sweetheart isn't so perfect, is she? I guess her and Ace are the best couple. They're perfect for each other."

Forgetting about himself, Ace ran off the stage, heading towards Amber. He tried to pull her to him, but she only backed away, turning and running into the crowd. Ace chased after her. Josh and Bambi exchanged looks, preparing to follow them.

"Speaking of relationships. Let me introduce you to my ex, Josh Davis."

Hearing his name, Josh froze. Bambi was the first to turn around. People gasped, as a picture of him being abused was shown. Bambi tried to prevent him from looking, but failed, as he moved her arms away. He stared at the screen emotionless, which scared Bambi. "Josh…"

"He was too embarrassed of me, but it looks like I should be the one embarrassed. I mean, who still gets beatings at eighteen?! Rich people problems, am I right?"

Thinking it was a joke and that Josh wasn't getting abused, people laughed. But, Bambi knew the truth. Josh had never said his father was abusive, but Bambi could tell from the picture, it wasn't just his father "disciplining" him. Josh didn't look at anyone, as he tried to escape the laughter.

"Which reminds me of my next subject. Bambi Johnson. The girl you all think is so innocent and sweet. And, is just always happy."

Bambi dropped her head, not believing all of this was happening. When she lifted her head, she felt her eyes water. A picture of her leaving the mental health center was displayed.

"Turns out she has more problems than any of us" Courtney laughed *"And that's the girl he left me for? Pathetic. Definitely a downgrade if you ask me."*

Bambi felt all eyes on her and her anxiety begin to kick in. She wanted to run, yet she couldn't move. She felt a tear fall from her eyes. This was a night she was supposed to always remember, now she wanted more than anything to forget it. Courtney wasn't finished, though.

"And last, but not least we have Captain of the cheerleading team, most popular, and prettiest girl in the school, Madison Williams or as some of you may know her, Gossip Guru."

A spotlight hit Madison and not only were there pictures of her, but videos too. Some showing her with men twice her age and others showing her arguing with her drunk mother outside of a club.

"The prettiest people live the ugliest lives."

The lights were turned back on and the music began to play. No one moved, though. Then, like a snap of the fingers, people began to whisper. Staring at all of them and even pointing. Some were even on their phone. No doubt posting all that happened. Soon, everyone in RoseOoak would know what happened tonight and all the secrets that were revealed. The others weren't used to the bullying and rumors like Bambi was. She was sure they were taking things hard.

Bambi looked on stage. Madison hadn't moved from her spot. Frozen. Like a deer in headlights. A camera flashed, as people began taking pictures of her. Madison snapped out of her daze, backing away. It was then Bambi noticed the tears running down her face. The crown fell from her head, as she ran off the stage.

Bambi looked around for the others. Ace stood in a corner with Amber, trying to get her to calm down. Her chest was heaving, as she cried. Ace, too on the verge of shedding a tear. Josh was on the floor a couple feet away from them. His back was against the wall, as he held the back of his head rocking a little. Bambi couldn't tell if he was crying or not. She turned away from the heartbreaking sight of her friends and sighed. *This is all my fault.*

High school,

The equivalent to hell,

It's the place where our true selves are undone,

Turning us into something we wished we had
never become.

CHAPTER FOURTEEN

High School

Madison walked up the steps to the school's entrance, pulling the hoodie from off her head. The weekend had passed and she had hoped what happened at prom night had been forgotten. She checked her surroundings, before dialing Tiffany's number. Only to be sent to voicemail once again. Blowing out a frustrated breath, Madison took one last look around and turned to enter the building. She kept her head down praying no one would notice her.

She had prayed to late.

The first whisper she ignored. The second made her wrap her arms around herself. With the third whisper came many more. Soon, the whispers turned to shouts. It wasn't long, before the entire hallway was filled with students yelling out insults to her.

"Ew! Look at what she's wearing!"

"I can't believe she pretended she was better than *any* of us!"

"She's more of a slut than Bambi was!"

"I still wouldn't mind sleeping with her. Shouldn't be hard with how easy she is."

"Omg, Jeff! You can't sleep with her! Who knows how many STDs she has?!"

Madison finally made it to her locker and looked up only to wish she hadn't.

No one likes you!
SLUT!
Call me I got $5
555-067
Kill Yourself

Water filled her eyes, as she read the notes. *Not again.* Without wasting a second, Madison reached up and tore down each sticky note. Ripping some up and throwing them to the ground.

Hearing giggles, Madison turned around coming face to face with a group of girls. Some being girls she had bullied herself in the past. Hastily, Madison wiped her tears away. It didn't help. They had already seen them.

One of the girls giggled and placed her hand to her chest. "Aww…look. She's crying." The leader of the girls crossed her arms and smirked. "Not so tough now, huh Madison?"

Madison tried to face forward and ignore the whispers, as she set in class. It was no use. She didn't seem to be the only one having trouble, though. Sitting a couple seats ahead of her was Amber. The usually flawless girl looked on the verge of having a meltdown. Some gave her worried looks, while others were happy to finally see RoseOak's sweetheart have problems.

In the past, Madison probably would have been one of those people. Happy to see someone else unhappy, because it helped make her life seem not so bad. But, things were different. She and Amber were both in the same predicament. With the pressure constantly placed on Amber to be perfect, she couldn't even imagine what she was going through right now.

The bell rang. Her classmates barely paid their teacher any attention, as they exited the room. Each one of them deep in their own conversations. No doubt gossiping about all that had happened prom night.

"Amber? A word please."

Madison paused as she exited the doorway and moved to stand out of sight.

"Yes, ma'am?"

Their teacher sighed. *"You know there are lots of rumors going around, right? Rumors involving you and your reputation."*

"Yes. I am aware."

"Well, then you should also be aware of how bad this looks. For both the school's and your parents' image. They must be so disappointed. You're RoseOak's sweetheart, Amber. You can't afford to make mistakes like this. You're supposed to be a role model. Someone students can look up to. I understand you're about to graduate and want to have fun. But, how about saving all that for college. People won't make such a big deal about it there. And, by then you'll already be in. But, for now. Try to do the right thing and keep your image untainted. For the school's and your parents' sake."

"I understand. I can assure you I won't make the same mistake, again."

"I expect you not to. Have a good day."

"You, as well."

Madison had been so focused on eavesdropping, she didn't notice Amber's voice get closer. They bumped into each other, as Amber rounded the corner. She dropped her things and reached to pick them up, while mumbling an apology.

Amber rose up and froze locking eyes with Madison. Her emotionless face instantly turned into a frown. "What? Trying to find another topic for your blog, to take the attention off of you?"

Madison shook her head "N-No. I-"

Amber didn't give her time to finish, before rolling her eyes and walking towards her. "Get a life Madison and stop trying to ruin all of ours." She bumped shoulders with her, as she passed.

Madison turned around, watching her leave, She wanted to call out to her, but didn't have the courage to. She only dropped her head, whispering. "I'm sorry…."

Laughter came to a cease, as Madison walked into the locker room. All of her so-called friends were huddled in a circle and looked to have been watching something on Stephanie's phone. neither one of them hadn't checked on her that night, neither one of them answered her phone calls over the weekend, and neither one of them looked happy to see her right now. What shocked her the most was to see Tiffany amongst them.

Stephanie stood up off one of the benches and strutted towards her. "I honestly wasn't expecting you to show up. Tiffany I owe you five bucks!" she said with a laugh. Madison looked in Tiffany's direction, but she looked away.

Stephanie placed her weight to one side and crossed her arms, looking Madison over. "Look at you. You're definitely not the same Madison anymore. We owe our thanks to whoever it was that exposed you prom night."

Stephanie squinted her eyes and took closer steps toward her "You tried pretending you were so high above all of us, but it was all a lie. Your parents are divorced, your mother is an alcoholic, and you sleep with countless of men who are probably twice your age. You disgust me! You should just do us all a favor and disappear!"

The other girls just listened, nodding along to everything. Stephanie then backed away and placed a finger to her chin in confusion. "And, what else did I forget…." She taunted.

Looking Madison in the eye, she grinned wickedly. "Oh, yeah. You're off the cheerleading team. We all represent RoseOak and take pride in our school. And, we can't have you messing up what we and others before us have worked so hard for."

Stephanie moved around Madison walking out of the locker room. "Try keeping your legs closed next time." The other girls stood up, following after Stephanie. All of them mumbling an insult. Tiffany just kept her head down. *It looks like Stephanie was their new leader, now.*

Madison was about to head to her locker to change, but paused hearing shouting. She rushed out of the locker room to see Josh and Ace fighting with Tatum and Maddox.

Bambi and Amber, along with other members of the football team tried to break them apart. While others watched on, entertained by the whole situation. Holding their phones out to record rather than help.

Tatum laughed, watching Josh be held back.

"Don't take your anger out on me! Why not save some of that for your father."

Bambi stopped Josh from lunging at him, again.

Someone came to stand beside her and she looked seeing it was Tiffany. Tiffany spoke before she could. "You know this is all your fault, right?" Madison felt her stomach drop. "This all started with you bullying Bambi, because of your stupid grudge. Then it turned into bullying everyone you thought was weaker than you. You know I was only trying so hard to be your friend, because I didn't want you bullying me either."

Tiffany clenched her fist and twisted around to face her fully. "I didn't want to pick on people or talk about them over the phone! I didn't like making up false gossip, ruining people's lives! I never wanted any of it, but like everyone else I was too scared of you to say something!" She took a deep breath and shook her head "We can never be friends again," Locking eyes with Madison, she spoke warningly "Stay away from me."

Madison looked around seeing some people had been listening to their conversation. Things were different. No one was no longer scared of Madison. So, instead of turning away they watched her, laughing and whispering.

She looked back across the gym. Coach Green had managed to calm everything down, but that still didn't fix things. Those loyal to Ace and Josh stood on one side. While those on Tatum's and Maddox's side stood on the other. Madison took in the scene and bit her lip. *Was this all my fault?*

The day was almost over and Madison hoped she could make it through her last two periods. She walked around the cafeteria looking for a place to sit. Her hope was waning, until she spotted an empty table. As she got closer, she noticed someone sitting there. Bambi.

The other girl sat at the table with her headphones in her ear, reading a book. *She really hasn't changed.* Madison felt the familiar tingling feeling in her stomach that she now recognized. Guilt. Recent events had helped her realize she had been wrong for treating Bambi the way she did. She had been so focused on revenge, she had forgotten what forgiveness was. Coming to a conclusion, she started to walk towards her target. She was going to make things right.

Someone stepped in her way, as others crowded around her. Madison rolled her eyes at Courtney's annoying smirk. She identified Stephanie and Tiffany as the additional girls. "Where do you think you're going?" Courtney questioned.

Madison's eyes shifted to Bambi and Courtney followed them. She faced Madison again and laughed

"You've got to be kidding me. You don't think the two of you can be friends after all the stuff you've done to her, do you?" Madison remained quiet, feeling the effects of Courtney's words.

Stephanie laughed "I'll take that as a no." Tiffany crossed her arms "Someone like Bambi would never be friends with someone like you."

Courtney flipped her hair and "Besides, it doesn't look like she needs you, anyway." Madison looked around them and Courtney was right. Bambi was no longer by herself. Amber, Ace and Josh had joined her at the table. Josh still looked upset over the fight and Bambi held his hand speaking to him. Amber and Ace also spoke to him.

"Roles have reversed. She has friends, now. She's popular and *you're* the outsider."

Out of nowhere, Stephanie knocked her tray out of her hands. This caused the entire cafeteria to go silent. People stopped their conversations to look at them. Madison made eye contact with Bambi, who was giving her a worried stare.

289

Madison looked down at her tray and Courtney walked over to her, whispering in her ear. "Do something about it."

A chair scraped against the ground, as Bambi stood from her seat. *No, this is my problem.* Madison gave Courtney one final glare, before running out of the cafeteria.

We all reach a breaking point in our lives,

But we need this,

Our breaking points help us decide,

Whether we're going to fight or forfeit.

CHAPTER FIFTEEN

Breaking Point

Bambi walked into her house, slamming the door shut. She allowed her head to fall back against it, as she tried to regulate her breathing. She felt helpless within everything that was happening. No matter how hard she tried or how happy she was, life always had a way of pulling her back down again.

The past was starting to repeat itself, but with an awful twist. It was no longer her that was being taunted. The taunting had now made its way to the very people it was afraid of. The popular people were being made into outsiders by their so-called friends.

Bambi knew the others weren't as strong as her when it came to situations like this. They weren't used to being on the other side of bullying. Stuff like this could make or break you. Bambi had been fortunate enough to make it out of her depression, but that had taken her years. She only hoped it didn't take her friends that long.

Josh doubled over in pain, as his father's fist connected with his abdomen once again. It had been like this since he had gotten home from prom. People saw his father as just disciplining him and didn't think too much of the pictures. That still didn't stop Josh's father from taken out his frustrations on him.

"Do you know how bad that picture made me look?!" Punch "You're lucky no one took it serious!" Punch "I could kill you right now!" *You already have.* Josh had given up on fighting back a long time ago. He never won and knew he never would. The verbal abuse his father gave him was just as strong as the blows of his fists.

But, he took them all without ever shedding a tear. That would only make his father more violent. The first time he had cried was the last time he had cried. That had also been the first time his father had ever hit him.

Eleven Years Ago

"Dad. I want mama."

His father sighed, placing his paper work down. He turned to his side, eyeing his son with an irritated look. "I already told you, Josh. I don't know where your mother is, okay? She left us. And, she's not coming back so stop asking for her."

Josh's eyes watered and his lips began to tremble. "But, I want mama. Please, can't you just try to find her?"

His father continued to ignore and that's when Josh began to cry harder. "Josh! What have I told you about that?! Toughen up! You are a boy! Boys don't cry so stop it!"

Josh didn't listen and continued to cry "I want mama! I know she didn't want to leave us. She was just scared. Maybe if you apologize and promise not to hit her anymore, she'll-"

His rambling was cut off, as his father's hand connected with his mouth. Josh fell onto the floor by the force of the backhand. He looked up with fear in his eyes, as his father stood up towering over him.

Suddenly, his father's foot connected with his side. "Shut up! You're just a child! You don't know what you're talking about! Your mother brought all that upon herself! She made me hit her! If she would have just listened, she would not have gotten hurt!"

With every shout, Josh's father kicked him. And, with every kick, Josh screamed out in pain.

"Dad! Please stop!" he cried.

This did nothing, but make his father kick harder. "I thought I told you to stop all that crying!"

Finally, out of exhaustion and agony. Josh was able to stop crying. Feeling himself go numb from the pain. He was silent and didn't move. Seeing this, his father stopped his abuse and fixed himself up, before crouching down to Josh's level.

"That'll teach you not to cry like you're five years old." He then stood up, grabbing his phone off the desk. His father checked his phone and a smirk took over his face. Josh knew it must have been one of his lady "friends".

"I've got to go. I expect you to be cleaned up by the time I get back." Josh still didn't respond not even being able to move. He couldn't feel anything.

His father paused at the door and called over his shoulder "Oh and Josh? If you try telling anyone about what happened, today. I'll make sure the next time you open your mouth, it's without teeth. What happens in this house stays in this house. Your mother chose to go against that and look where she's at. Homeless. I'm sure you don't want that, so be smart. And, next time I say not to do something. Don't do it!"

His father left the office, slamming the door behind him. Josh still remained on the floor. Feeling as if he was close to death. A picture on the wall caught his eye and his eyes watered once again. He tried reaching his hand up, but it was too painful. "Mama...."

Present Day

Up until that day, Josh had always looked up to his father as his hero. He learned quickly that he was no such thing. A hero didn't steal from the poor to give to the rich. A hero didn't beat on the weak to feel stronger. A hero didn't seek pain to feel pleasure. His father wasn't a hero nor would he ever be.

Ace sat at the dinner table with his parents. No one speaking. His father would not even look at him since prom night. His mother had cried and tried persuading him to sign up for a drug program. Ace had refused it. He wasn't an addict. There wasn't any satisfaction when he would take the steroids. It made him feel worse if anything. But, that didn't stop him from taking them. He had to, in order to be the best.

The ringing of the house phone interrupted the uncomfortable silence. His father stood up from the table and walked over to it.

"Hello? Yes, this is he....Yes, and we are working on it....I know what it looks like, but...Yes, I understand....We would really appreciate it if you reconsidered, this was just a mere mistake...Yes...Yes, I understand sir...Thank you...You have a good day too, sir."

Ace shared a looked with his mother, as his father ended the call. His mother stood up from the table heading in his direction. "Sweetheart?" Out of nowhere, his father grabbed the house phone, throwing it in Ace's direction.

He was quick enough to dodge it, as his mother looked at the father with wide eyes. "What is wrong with you?! You could have hurt him-"

His father ignored his wife's ranting as he began to shout at him. "Another one! That's the second one this week.

People are taken away their offers and scholarships, because of a mistake you made. Soon, no one's going to want you! And, then you're going to be a nobody. You'll be lucky enough to coach the little leagues!"

Ace stood up from the table, fed up with his father "No! That's you, dad! That's your life! You had to settle for being a coach, because you chose to only focus on football. You chose to make football your only life! But, me?! I have other options! Football isn't the only thing I'm good at!"

His father took long strides toward him, with his mother trying to stop him. "And, what are you going to be a doctor?! Huh, Ace! They don't expect kids like you to be doctors! That's for the kids that got something! The one's that come from something! We're not even middle class! Football is where the success is! That's going to take you far. Not wasting eight years of your life for a job you might not even get!"

Ace began to block out what his father was saying, feeling a headache come on. His father would never see things his way. He would never support his dreams, because they weren't his own.

The shouting grew louder and his headache began to get worse. Ace's vision was becoming blurry and he could no longer hear or understand his father's words. There was a strange taste in his mouth and he felt himself losing control of his body. Before he knew it, he was falling.

"Ace?!"

He felt his father catch him, but couldn't move. The last thing he heard was his mother screaming and his father shouting his name.

Rain fell, but Madison ignored it. Her mind was too clouded to even feel it. Her arms were wrapped around herself, as she shook. But, not from the cold.

Two hours ago

Madison entered the house with tears streaming down her face. She could hear laughter coming from her mother's room and closed her eyes in anger. She would always question why life had to be this way. Why was she always suffering? What did she do to deserve this life?

Things were different, now. She could no longer go to school and take out her problems and frustrations on everybody else. She was going to have to deal with everything on her own.

She placed her bag down and went to sit on the couch, pulling out her phone. Normally she would just lock herself in her room, but she didn't feel like hearing her and her mother's company.

A door opened and the smell of smoke made its way into the living room. Madison looked up, as Frank appeared out of the hallway. She frowned and focused her attention back on her phone. When she looked up again, she could see Frank heading towards the kitchen. Probably for another beer. Madison rolled her eyes at the pathetic man.

She heard the refrigerator door close and footsteps. A body sat down next to hers. Madison sat up and locked eyes with Frank, quickly placing her legs down. She made sure her hoodie was zipped up all the way and Frank noticed this.

He tilted his head and reached out a finger to touch her zipper. "What's up with the new look-"

Madison didn't let him finish slapping his hand away. "Don't touch me!" she shrieked in disgust, hoping her mother would hear her.

Frank only smirked, leaning back on the couch. His eyes roamed her body. "You look just like your mother, you know? Just younger and prettier." He set his beer down, scooting closer to her. "I'm not that much older than you, you know. I'm only twenty-five. Your mother's okay, but a woman gets boring after a while, you know? You'll be eighteen soon-"

"No!" Madison shouted pushing his hand away. She recognized the look in his eyes and it made her skin crawl. It was the same look the others gave her, but she no longer

wanted to be that girl. She didn't want to be viewed that way either.

Madison stood up and tried to walk away "I'm going to my room." Only to have frank pull her back down. She tried to pull her arm away, but his grip on her was too tight. "Let go!"

Frank squeezed her arm tighter "Shut up! You can stop playing innocent. We both know the truth. I've seen the looks you've been giving me."

Madison shook her head and tried to pull her arm away, again. "You're sick! Let me go! Mom!" she cried, hoping her mom would come to her rescue. She knew where things were headed.

Frank covered her mouth with his freehand and pushed her onto the couch. His body covered hers. "Your mom doesn't have to know." Madison began to kick wildly, as he placed a kiss on her neck. In that moment she wished she could die. Anything would be better than what was happening to her.

Just as Frank moved to unbuckle his pants, Madison's mother appeared. She frowned taking in the scene and screamed "What is going on?!" Frank jumped off of Madison and she rushed over to her mother. Clinging to her, as tears fell down her face. "He...He tried to rape me!" she shouted, pointing to Frank.

He shook his head, holding his hands up. "Baby, she's lying. I would never do something like that. She came onto me, first. She said she needed money-"

Madison grabbed a cd and threw it at him "You're a liar!"

Frank shot her a glare and returned his eyes to her mother. "Baby, who are you going to believe? I'm the one that gives you money and pay the bills. You're the only woman I want. She's just lying to get money out of me and get us both in trouble. If she goes to the cops, we'll both be put in jail. Come on, we both know how she is. She just wants some attention."

Her mother didn't respond and Madison whirled around to face her. She took her mother's hands, but she

continued to stare forward. Her face was emotionless.
"Mom?" Madison begged, trying to get her to look at her.

"Mom?!"

Her mother looked at her and that's when Madison realized her mother was gone. She had no clue when her mother had disappeared, but the woman that was now glaring at her was not her mother.

Snatching her hands away, her mother's hand connected with her cheek. Madison's head whipped to the side and she reached her hand up to hold the stinging area.

"M-Mom...."

Tears filled in her eyes, as she watched her mother stare at her with so much hate. "Get out!" she said pointing to the door. She pushed Madison toward it, causing her to lose her balance a little. "Get out, you little slut!" Madison backed away, as her mother grew closer. "Every man! Every man that comes into my life, you drive them away! Not this time! This time I'm going to get rid of the problem! Which is you! So, get out!"

Madison felt her throat closing up. She couldn't believe her mother was going to actually kick her out. Where was she going to go?

Unconsciously, her eyes wondered back to Frank. He avoided eye contact with her. Madison glared at him. Her attention was brought back onto her mother, as she received another slap. "Last time, get out!"

Madison ran to the couch, grabbing her phone. She ran to the door and picked up her bag. "I hate you!" she screamed, before leaving, shutting the door on her way out.

Present

Now, here she was sitting on the bridge, as she felt herself at her breaking point. There was just too much bad in her life. She had come to the conclusion that she wasn't one of those girls that got a happily ever after. She didn't deserve one either. Tonight she was going to do the town a favor. There was just one last thing she needed to do, first. One last person she needed to speak to. There was an apology that was long overdue. She just hoped the number was the same.

Amber rushed to her room and slammed the door shut. She kicked off her shoes and snatched her hair out of the bun it was in. She walked around the room, snatching the pictures off the wall. She was sick of everything. Sick of school, sick of her parents, and sick of the stupid town! No one ever cared about her. They didn't worry for her mental health. Never asked if she was okay. She was just one human being! Too many people expected too much from her.

"Amber what is all that noise?! Quiet down!"

She ignored her mother's voice. Still not satisfied, Amber walked around the room destroying every award, medal, and trophy she had ever gotten. Destroying everything that had caused her pain.

Her room was destroyed, but Amber still didn't feel any better. Amber looked to her bathroom and knew what she had to do. This would solve all her problems. It didn't feel as if she was in control of her body, as she walked toward the bathroom. Everything seemed to fade away. She couldn't see anything, but the medicine cabinet.

One pill wouldn't do anything. Two pills wouldn't stop the thoughts. Three pills wouldn't be enough. Three pills were never enough. Amber emptied the entire bottle into her hand and placed the pills into her mouth. She turned on the sink faucet and cupped a hand full of water. Using the water, she swallowed the pills. No one truly knew her. No one truly loved her. No one saw the girl behind the mask. *And she wouldn't give them the chance to.*

The pills were starting to kick in and she walked out of the bathroom into her bedroom. The faucet was left running. Her vision was blurred and her footsteps started to fumble. Her legs soon caved and she fell onto the floor. She felt her body become heavy and could no longer feel her limbs. Amber felt her eye lids fall and did not fight the urge to sleep. Before her eye's closed she heard her brother's frightened voice

"Amber?!"

Bambi's phone rang and she used the remote to turn the T.V. down. Her eyebrows furrowed, wondering who would call her this late. An unknown number appeared on her screen. A strange chill ran up her spine. She was going to ignore it, but something told her not to.

"Hello?"

Sniffling could be heard over the phone, making Bambi worried. "Hello?" she tried again, hoping the person would respond.

"Bambi?"

Bambi sat up in her bed, eyes wide. "Madison?" she questioned in disbelief. Not believing that she had actually called her. The other girl laughed. *"Still haven't changed your number, I see."*

Bambi didn't respond for a while. She was trying to wrap her head around why Madison would be calling her, especially at night.

Madison sighed into the phone, before speaking.

"I know you probably don't want to hear this, right now. Especially with what's going on. But, I just want you to know that I'm sorry, Bambi,"

"I was wrong for bullying you and I understand that, now. And, I can't apologize enough for what I've done to you. But, I was angry. I was angry at the kids at school, I was angry at my mom, but I don't want to feel this way anymore. I don't want to feel anything at all, anymore. I just want this pain and anger to end..."

Bambi's heart dropped. She could hear the pain in Madison's voice and it honestly frightened her. The way Madison was speaking, was as if she had already given up. The sound of cars honking could be heard and Bambi frowned.

"Madison, where are you?"

The line went silent for a while and Bambi checked to see if the call had dropped. Madison's number still was on the screen, and so she waited for a response. "Madison?"

"Goodbye, Bambi."

The line went dead and that's when Bambi began to panic. Her heart pounded against her chest. She tried dialing the number back, but it only went to voicemail.

Five years ago

Bambi leaned over and placed her hands on her knees. She lifted her head to glance up over at Madison. She was breathing heavily, tears still streaming down her face. Bambi felt bad for her friend. They had ran all the way from Madison's house, when her parents had begun to fight.

The two of them had crawled out of Madison's bedroom window. Madison had taken off running, before Bambi could even speak. It didn't take her long to follow after her friend. They didn't stop running, until Madison had become tired.

Bambi stood up and looked around, not recognizing her surroundings. Madison followed her. She turned to look at Bambi, her eyebrows knitted together. "Where are we?"

Shrugging whilst crossing her arms, Bambi scowled "How am I supposed to know? I was following you!" Madison grinned and laughed, wiping at her face. She took in their surroundings once again and smiled at her friend.

Bambi arms fell at her side, as she slowly backed away from the creepy smile on her friend's face. "What are you doing…?"

Out of nowhere, Madison grabbed Bambi's hand.

"This is our safe spot. Whenever one of us is going through something, let's come here. Okay?"

"Okay."

Present Day

Bambi now had an idea of where Madison could possibly be, now she just had to find a way to get to her. She tried calling Amber and Ace, but they too went to voicemail. The last person she tried was Josh. Thankfully, on the third ring, Josh answered.

"Yes?"

His voice sounded different over the phone. Almost like it was a strain on him.

"Are you okay?"

"Yeah?"

"Josh...."

"Come on, Bambi. Let's not get into this. What do you need?"

Bambi bit back wanting to find out what was really going on with him and got to the point.

"It's Madison."

"Yeah? What about her?"

"Something's wrong. I think she's in danger."

"Yeah. She's finally going to get what she deserved."

"Josh, I think she's going to kill herself."

It sounded as if Josh dropped the phone. It took a few seconds of rumbling, before he could speak again.

"Are you sure? What would make you think that? Madison is one of the most confident people in the school."

"She's still human, Josh. She called me a few minutes ago. Saying she was sorry and that she was sick of being angry and in pain. She said she doesn't want to feel anything. I heard cars in the background, come on, this is serious, Josh!"

He was quiet for a while.

"Do you know where she could be?"

"Yeah, just come get me. I don't know how long we have."

Bambi hung up the phone and began to place on more suitable clothing. It was late at night, so she knew her mother would not allow her to go out. Thankfully, she was asleep. Bambi hoped she could sneak out without her waking up.

Bambi quickly ran to Josh's car. She kept her head down. Even though her neighbors were elderly and probably asleep by now, she still didn't want to take that chance.

She entered Josh's car and hastily placed on her seatbelt with shaking hands. Josh chuckled from beside her "Why are you wearing all black?" Bambi frowned, looking down in her attire. "Hello? We're sneaking out here." She then looked him over. "Wait. Why *aren't* you wearing all black?"

Josh chuckled and shook his head, reaching to start the ignition. Bambi's eyes widened. His shirt's sleeve had rolled up, revealing the bruises he had tried to conceal. He caught this and hurriedly fixed his sleeve. He started up the car and proceeded to drive, not making eye contact.

"Josh-"

"I don't want to talk about it, Bambi."

She didn't push it, knowing it must have been hard for him. No man wanted to appear weak, especially in front of a woman. Bambi wished Josh knew that she didn't see him that way. If anything, she equalized his weakness to pain. In the past, Josh had done a good job at hiding it from everyone. But, she knew the truth. Which made it even more heartbreaking to watch him deal with his pain alone.

"Stop the car!" Bambi screeched, causing Josh to slam on the breaks. The car jerked, before coming to a stop.

"Is that Madison?!"

Bambi didn't respond to his question. Still shocked by what she was seeing. Snapping out of her daze, she hurriedly unbuckled her seatbelt and exited the car.

"Bambi, wait-"

Josh's words were ignored. Bambi slowly made her way toward Madison. Every part of her body was uneasy. Part of her wished she had called for help, but she didn't know how Madison would react to it.

The most popular girl in school. The life that was envied by most of the school. The false happiness people *wished* they had. The girl everyone wanted or wanted to be was now sitting on a bridge ready to take her life at any given moment.

Bambi stopped, once she was a couple feet away from Madison. A car door slammed and Bambi twisted around to see Josh exiting his car. He gave her a worried look and she returned it. She took a deep breath, before speaking.

"Madison-"

"You shouldn't have come here."

Bambi flinched at her tone. It came out harsh, yet sounded full of pain and exhaustion.

"Madison, please don't do this," Bambi begged. "Things don't have to go this far. You might think that taking your life is the only way out, but you're wrong. I know how you're feeling-"

She was cut off by a cruel laugh. "You know how I feel?" Madison glanced over her shoulder to glare at her "You don't have a clue as to what I am feeling! Yeah, I get it! I bullied you, okay! And, I apologize for that, but comparing our pains is wrong! They're not the same! At the end of the day, you have a safe place to go to! You have someone that loves and cares for you! I have nobody! School was my only safe place! Now, I don't even have *that*! Instead I have to go home to my alcoholic mother and her alcoholic friends, who can't keep their hands to themselves!"

Tears were running down her face, as she vented out her frustrations.

Bambi felt her eyes water, but pushed it away. This was about Madison not her. She felt her mouth shake, trying to get the words out. "Madison? D-Did he r-r-ra-"

She was once again, cut off by a dark laugh. Madison laughed and wiped away her tears. "Nope. He was going to, though. Can you believe it? In a matter of seconds, I was going to be a victim. While my mother was only a couple feet away, but was too stuck in her world that she didn't notice mine was about to be destroyed…"

Another flow of tears began, but she still kept the broken smile on her face. "She walked in on it. He jumped off me and I ran to her. I threw my arms around her and hugged her tight. My eyes were closed. I was still a little shaken up from it, but I remember feeling safe in her arms. I thought *finally*. Finally, she'll be the mother I needed her to be. She'll go to rehab and things would get better. Boy, was I wrong."

Her hands clenched onto the bridge's railing and her face was now pulled into a frown. "He blamed me. He said that I came onto him. And, she believed him. She believed him over me! Her own daughter! She kicked me out for a man she barely knew!" Her voice cracked with despair.

"Why couldn't she just be a mother? She didn't need to be perfect. Just a mother. That's all I wanted…"

Madison used her arm to wipe her face and turned back around to face the traffic below them. "Don't compare our pains, Bambi. Trust me, they're not the same."

"Madison, I'm sorry you had to go through that, but this is not the answer. We can get you help. *This* is not the answer!"

Her once best friend, gave her a slight smile, before shaking her head. "I'm sorry, Bambi."

"Madison, no…"

"I'm sorry."

And, with her final words being said. She closed her eyes and pushed off the railing, accepting whatever her fate was. Anything was better than living.

We hold our breath,

Just as we hold in our pain,

Until we just stop breathing completely,

But deep inside we have that one breath that's left,

So fight,

Fight for what's best, fight for life instead of death.

CHAPTER SIXTEEN

Breathe

Madison opened her eyes, confused. They widened once they connected with Bambi's. There was a strained look on the girl's face, as she held on to Madison's arm tight. Once Madison realized what Bambi was doing, she began fighting against her.

"Madison, stop! My grip is slipping!"

"Let me go!"

"No!"

The two of them fought against each other. Both using all of their strength.

Bambi's next words caused Madison to freeze.

"Think of Peyton!"

They locked eyes and Bambi continued, tears streaming down her face.

"No one fought for him, Madison! That's why he's gone, because no one fought for him, but I'm fighting for you, but I can't do it alone. You've got to meet me half way, okay. Please, don't give up. This isn't the end. High school isn't the end. There's so much more. College, Careers, Love, Family, Retirement. Life!" Bambi choked on her words and tightened her grip. "Please, fight Madison, please..."

Madison battled with her thoughts. For the past few months, she hadn't seen anything beyond high school. She didn't think of high school or her future. To her this was it. There was nothing to look forward to. She didn't know who she was outside of RoseOak. How could she look forward to life when she didn't know how to live it?

She looked up at Bambi and could see the pleading look in her eyes. Tears rushed to her eyes. After everything,

Bambi was still here as if nothing had happened between them. *Maybe, I could try again.*

Using all of her strength, Madison used her other hand to grab onto Bambi's arm. She saw that as confirmation and began to pull her up. They both fell to the ground and before Madison could react, Bambi threw her arms around her sobbing. Madison followed after her. Both of them clinging onto one another. No longer enemies.

"I don't know if I can do this, Bambi" Madison mumbled into her shoulder, feeling her doubt start to surface again. Bambi pulled away from her, but held her at arm's length. "Yes, you can. You've just got to want it for your-self. The moment you tell yourself you *can*, you *will*. And, I'll be there for you. You're not in this alone, Madison."

She smiled and opened her mouth to say something, but stopped once she spotted Josh. He ran up to them, look-ing panicked. Bambi stood up and scowled "Where were you! Things could have went-"

His breathing was ragged and he looked as if he was going to be sick. Bambi's face went from anger to concern Josh was barely able to get his words out. *"Hospital..."*

Bambi placed her hands on his face and made him look at her. "Josh, look at me. What's wrong?"

He squeezed his eyes shut and took deep breaths. "Hospital...Amber and Ace...Things don't look good. We've got to go." He finished, before running off.

Bambi and Madison shared worried looks, before following after him.

Madison shifted uncomfortably, as Ace and Amber's parents' cried. Josh and Bambi tried consoling them, but nothing was working. Madison couldn't begin to imagine the pain they were feeling. She wished her own mother would care for her the way they did their children.

These events had also made her realize, she wasn't the only one living a fake life. Amber-RoseOak's sweetheart had overdosed and was now fighting for her life. The worst part was that it had been her little brother to find her. He was probably going to be scarred for the rest of his life. Ace-the school's star athlete had a seizure and was in the same predicament as Amber. It was kind of ironic. Sort of like Romeo and Juliet. Madison just hoped their story didn't end the same way.

"This is all my fault."

Madison looked over at Mr. Hart who had finally spoken, after minutes of silence and blank staring. His wife took his hand in hers. "It's both our faults. We put too much pressure on her."

"What have I done?" Mr. Hart questioned and broke down right then and there. Seeing the usually stoic man cry was both terrifying and heartbreaking.

Mr. Woods spoke up from where he was seated. He glanced at his wife who still wasn't speaking to him and sighed. His eyes were red and puffy. He ran a hand down his face and spoke. "I guess I'm in the wrong, just as much as you guys are. I just wanted him to be better than me, you know? I didn't want him to struggle like I did. I wanted him to live the life I never got a chance to. Maybe, that was the problem. I was making him live my life instead of his. Now, my son's fighting something I caused."

The sound of footsteps caught everyone's attention. Two doctors walked into the room. One wearing a reassuring smile and the other a sympathetic one. Madison wondered who the sympathetic doctor would be delivering the bad news to.

The reassuring doctor took a step forward "Parents of Ace Woods?" Mr. and Mrs. Wood rushed toward the doctor. "Is Ace, okay?" Mrs. Wood said, practically begging them to say yes.

The doctor nodded "Yes. He's in stable condition, now. We've got everything under control. In an hour he should be up and you'll be able to see him."

You could see the weight lift off their shoulders, as they thanked the doctor.

The sympathetic doctor took a step forward and everyone became silent, waiting for his news. "Mr. and Mrs. Hart." They stepped forward, slowly. The looks on their faces told as if they already knew what to expect. Probably noticing the doctor's expression like Madison had.

The doctor sighed. "This isn't easy to say, so I'm just going to come right out with it. Amber isn't doing so well. Her heart stopped a couple times, luckily we were able to revive it, but she's fallen into a coma. There's nothing we can do, but have hope. There's a high chance that if she doesn't come out of her coma in the next twenty-four hours, she'll become brain dead. I'm sorry."

As soon as, his words were out, Mrs. Hart let out a scream of anguish. She fell to the ground, but was caught by Mr. Woods. Mr. Hart took a couple steps backwards, before fainting.

Madison realized she had been foolish in her earlier decision. Things may be hard, but it wasn't worth taking her life over. Two people who had their whole lives ahead of them were in the hospital and one of them was barely holding on. Death was proving to be much scarier than she thought.

"Courtney, wake up!"

A voice yelled, just as she was hit in the arm hard. She yelped and jumped out of her sleep. Her fright turned to annoyance. Candice stood next to her bed, hovering over her with a menacing look.

"What do you want?" Courtney groaned and turned over. She pulled her comforter over her head, trying to go back to sleep, but Candice snatched it off her completely.

Courtney sat up in her bed, throwing a pillow at her older sister. "What's your problem?!" Candice picked the pillow up, before throwing it back at her hard. She pointed to the hallway and whispered, angrily.

"Lower your voice! The cops are here and they're looking for *you*!"

Courtney felt fear come over her. She had been doing a lot of stuff the past months and wondered if things were catching up to her.

She glanced up at her sister and gulped "D-Did they say what they wanted?"

Candice crossed her arms and shook her head "No, but it's most likely nothing serious. Probably a couple lost textbooks from freshmen year. They'll just give mom a certain amount of time to pay it off, before you graduate or put it on her credit. Nothing to stress over." She stated with a wave of her head, while picking at her nails.

Courtney nodded and got out of her bed. She followed Candice into the hallway and noticed all her younger siblings' heads poking out their rooms, watching. They walked down the stairs and Courtney stomach fell, as she laid eyes on the police officers. Their faces were expressionless and something in her gut told her things weren't right.

Her mother gave her a tried, scolding look and turned to the police officers. "Okay, as you can see, she's here. Now, can you tell me what this is all about?"

The bigger officer blew out a breath "Ma'am, Your daughter is a suspect in a recent robbery. She and a couple other teenagers were caught on tape, yesterday. We've also found drugs and alcohols in her lockers at school. So, if the robbery doesn't cost her to do time *that* will."

Courtney's mother placed a hand to her heart, looking as if she was going to pass out. She fell backwards, but Candice caught her. Their mother began to cry and Candice glared at Courtney, accusingly.

"Mom, I…"

"Please, place your hands behind you back. Anything you do or say can be used against you…"

The officer's words trailed off, as Courtney focused on her mother. The feel of the handcuffs caused tears to surface to her eyes. "Mom? Mom, look at me! Please! I'm sorry!"

Just then, the television made an alarm sound. Which meant there was an important message. Everyone focused their attention there and waited. A woman appeared on the screen. She looked distressed by the news, herself. She cleared her throat, before speaking.

"RoseOak's sweetheart, Amber Hart. Daughter of Arthur and Savannah Hart state has just been released..." Sighs. *"She has now fallen into a coma. Her chances of survival are very thin. Doctors say she has only twenty-four hours left to pull through, before she is pronounced brain dead. A couple hours ago, the young girl overdosed on what appeared to be illegal stress pills that were called back three years ago. Officials suspect her overdose has something to do with the recent stress of a prank pulled on a couple students during prom. Which proceeded to expose things going on in each students' personal lives..."*

Courtney felt her heart drop. *Amber was in the hospital?* Her best friend was on the verge of passing and it was all her fault. Things weren't meant to go this far and she now regretted all the things she had done.

The cops snapped out of their daze, appearing to be distrust over the news. Her mother still wouldn't look at her. Candice was giving her sympathetic look.

"Mama? Where's Courtney going? Why are you guys crying?"

Courtney looked up to see her siblings all watching her with crying and confused faces, as she was ushered away from them. The officers led her over to the car and placed her in. Her family stood at the front door, as the officers pulled off. Courtney's head fell along with tears. She was afraid of what the future held for her. Courtney wished more than anything that she could change things. But, it was too late. She hadn't thought about her actions, now she was going to have to suffer the consequences.

A Popular Outsider,

Both noticed and ignored,

Often envied by most,

But never comforted,

Few choose to be themselves,

Few can be themselves,

But that's what makes a Popular Outsider unique.

EPILOGUE

Popular Outsiders

It was graduation day, and a lot of things had happened since then. Miraculously, Amber had woken up from her coma. She had spent the last couple of weeks healing and was able to attend graduation with the rest of her classmates. Her parents were no longer putting pressure on her to be perfect. She was still going to attend RoseOak University, but would be going there to study for the career *she* had chosen. Which was to be a veterinarian. This had shocked everyone. It seemed the farm had made an impact on her.

Ace was still recovering from his seizure and wouldn't be able to play for a couple months. He was nevertheless granted his scholarship, though and planned to play football in college. But, his main goal was to use his scholarship for something he deemed more important. Ace didn't want to rely on football his whole life and decided to study medicine with hopes in becoming a neurosurgeon. He would be the first doctor in his family.

Josh was no longer staying with his father. Mr. Woods had seen his bruises at the hospital and confronted him on it. Once he knew what was going on behind closed doors, he demanded Josh leave his father's custody. He had offered Josh a place at his home, but he refused. By then Coach Green had gotten word of the matter. He was able to convince Josh to move in with him and his wife. Josh had agreed. And, the whole thing turned out to be a blessing for all three of them. Coach Green and his wife were never able to have children, so they were more than happy to take Josh in. And, Josh finally had the family he deserved.

Madison was no longer known as Gossip Guru. She had given up her role as the school's queen bee and decided to just be herself. She had some credits to catch up on, which she planned on doing over the summer. After that, she was going to go to cosmetology school. She thought of this as a way to put her skills to use. She was staying with Ms. Clover and it had a great effect on the both of them. Both needed each other to deal with their depression and pain. Ms. Clover had lost her child, but she had gained one as well.

Bambi had decided to study to become a therapist. This year had gave her a better viewpoint on life. People needed real help and she wanted to save as many lives as she could. She along with the rest of her friends had created a program for the summer. It was supposed to help them and others deal with their depression and suicidal thoughts. She was really looking forward to it. It had taken a lot of planning and hard work, but it was all worth it in the end.

Almost losing two of the most loved teenagers had woken the town up. People were starting to see that bullying was no joke and it was time to take action and change things.

"And, now a word from a two of our students and faculty member. Ms. Clover, Madison and Bambi."

The crowd cheered and Bambi snapped out of her thoughts. They all stood up and walked over to the podium. Ms. Clover was the first to speak.

"Hello, my name is Patricia Clover. Some of you may know me as Ms. Clover-your children's school counselor. Earlier this year, I lost my son and only child to bullying. He hung himself," Everyone in the crowd wore grieving expressions. *"I was just like all of you. If someone would have told me my child was suicidal, I would have laughed and called them crazy. In my eyes, I gave my child all the love and care that he needed, but that wasn't enough. I gave him what I thought was best for him. My job was making sure students were okay, especially with their mental health. But, I wasn't able to do that with my own son and in the end I lost him."*

"First, it started off with his stuff always coming up missing. He would come home with scratches and bruises. When I would ask him about it he would lash out. I now realized that was just a defense mechanism. In reality, he was just crying out for help. He made excuses to why he couldn't go to school. His grades started to slip and

338

he no longer took interest in his school work. There was always complaints and problems with his looks as if he was insecure with himself. He seemed moody all the time and his emotions would be all over the place. I passed it off as him just being a normal teenager, but I was wrong."

Ms. Clover took a breath and tears filled her eyes. *"My son's gone and there's nothing I can do to change that. But, maybe I can help some of you that still have a chance. Pay attention to your children. Live for them and not for yourselves. Stop putting pressure on them to be what you want them to be. Let them live out their dreams and make sure you're giving them the care they deserve. First depression comes and then suicide. And, trust me, you don't want it to get that far. Thank You."*

The crowd was quiet, but then everyone began to clap and cheer. Giving Ms. Clover a standing ovation.

Next, it was Madison's turn. She looked nervous, so Bambi gave her hand a reassuring squeeze. She replaced Ms. Clover at the podium and waited until the crowd was finished.

"I was a bully," Some of the parents in the crowd frowned and students began to whisper. *"Might have even bullied some of your children and I apologize for that. I would be lying if I said I had nothing to do with Peyton's death. Wanting to fit in with others and remain acknow-ledged, I bullied him along with everyone else. No bully expects their victims to really kill themselves, but Peyton did. We had pushed him too far and taken a child away from their mother. Thankfully, she was able to find it in her heart to forgive,"* Madison glanced over at her and smiled. Ms. Clover returned it.

"I came from a broken home. My parents divorced when I was in middle school and my mom turned to alcohol for comfort. Home seemed like the equiva-lent to hell. And, I hated knowing at the end of the day that was where I would be going. To keep my real life a secret, I created a false one. I pretended I was living the perfect life and had everything I needed. In truth, I would have traded lives with anyone of you. At home, I was the bully victim. So, I came to school to change that."

"Bullies never bully just, because it's fun. Nine times out of ten they bully for power. The feeling of being above someone, because everywhere else you're nothing. I belittled others to feel superior. Prom night, my true life was exposed and I was back to being inferior. It also helped me realize what I was doing was wrong. The shoe was on the other foot,"

She paused, before struggling to say her next sentence.

"A couple weeks ago, I tried to commit suicide."

Bambi's eyes widened and she shared a look with Ms. Clover. The older woman was at a loss for words, as was the rest of the crowd. No one had knew about Madison's suicide attempt, but Josh and Bambi. She was shocked that Madison was brave enough to admit something so personal.

"But, a friend of mine was able to stop me. She convinced me that there was something to look forward to. That high school wasn't the final destination and she was right. High School isn't our final destination. There's so

much more in life to look forward to and the only way we'll be able to achieve that is by living. Thank you."

Once again, the crowd cheered. Bambi was zoned out still in disbelief of Madison declaration. How could she follow up, after *that*? Madison walked toward Bambi and nodded to the podium. She gave her a little push and Bambi smiled at her in gratitude. She looked throughout the crowd, spotting her mother and friends. Their smiles encouraged her.

"Um, hi. My name's Bambi. I think it's safe to say every one of us in here has been a victim of bullying. I guess you could say that it's a part of life, but the thing is it doesn't have to be. Can't we all enjoy one another without tearing each other down? It may seem like a joke in your eyes, but bullying hurts. In order to not seem weak and be picked on even more, we hide our pain. We cry in privacy and try to exile ourselves from the world."

"This can lead to dangerous things and not just suicide. There have been many who decide to deal with their pain by afflicting it on others. School shootings for

example. Which causes people who were innocent in the matter to lose their lives as well."

"To those who are bully victims, I beg you not to give up. Bullies become bullies with the power you give them. A bully can gain control over hundreds of students, yet no one is brave enough to stand up to them. I'm not saying do anything that can get you hurt, but don't just sit around and continue to suffer. Tell an adult. If you're afraid of the backlash you might get, do it anonymously. It is fear that stops us. Fear of being bullied more, fear of being the next target, or the fear of being shunned by others. This needs to stop! Or else, children and teens will continue to fear the second place their supposed to feel the safest. Bullying has to come to a stop and we've come up with a way to stop it."

Bambi nodded for the men to drop the covering. It fell revealing the banner. People followed her gaze and looked behind them. Gasps rang out. Bambi smiled and continued speaking.

"We introduce to you all our new campaign, banning bullying. In dedication to Peyton Smith, we present you, The Popular Outsider Campaign!"

People stood up and began to clap while cheering. The field was full of shouts and whistles. Bambi waited for them to calm down, before saying her closing message.

"A Popular Outsider. Both noticed and ignored. Often envied by most. But, never comforted. Few choose to be themselves. Few can be themselves. But, that's what makes a Popular Outsider unique. Embrace your Popular Outsider…"

Author's Note

Firstly, I would like to thank you all for reading my novel. Out of all the writing I have done, this project is the one I'm most proud of. I feel **Popular Outsiders** is a book for everyone. It tackles a lot of things for Parents. Parents who are dealing with bullied children and parents who have lost their children to the hands of bullying.

But, the main thing this book focuses on is both the bully and the bully victim. I know some people may find this off putting, but I think it was interesting to actually get the bully's side to bullying. Which would be Madison and others. Doing this also helped me come to a better understanding of my bullies and actually forgive them. Most of the time we just think bullies are born evil or treat *everyone* cruelly. But, bullies can often be the victims themselves sometimes. And, this book touches on that.

Now, onto the bully victim which would be Bambi. Writing Bambi's character was very deep to me and often hard to write. When writing her character, I had to go deep into my past. I wanted Bambi's character to go through true bullying experiences. At times it was hard for me to write, because it felt like I was reliving it. But, it also helped me. I was able to finally face my past and cope with it. Most bully victims think they're alone and Popular Outsiders lets them know that they are not.

Please if you're experiencing any of these things seek out help. Do not try to face your problems alone.

26317526R00209

Made in the USA
Columbia, SC
12 September 2018